A

Peter Dickinson was born in the Victoria Falls. When he was seven, his family moved to England, where he later graduated from Cambridge. For seventeen years he worked on the staff of the magazine *Punch* before starting his career as a writer – which he knew he was meant for since he was five years old. His first book was published in 1968, and since then he has written more than fifty novels for adults and young readers. In 1999 he was one of three writers chosen for the shortlist for Britain's first Children's Laureate, and in 2000 he was shortlisted for the International Hans Christian Andersen Award.

Among his award-winning children's books are *City of Gold* (Carnegie Medal), *Tulku* (Carnegie Medal and Whitbread Children's Book of the Year), *Eva* (Highly Commended for the Carnegie Medal) and *The Blue Hawk* (Guardian Children's Fiction Award). *AK* won the Whitbread Children's Book of the Year Award.

Praise for *AK*:

'A powerful story, alive with the smells and colours and rhythms of Africa.'
*The Bookseller*

'A novel of considerable tension and pace.'
*TES*

'Peter Dickinson at his best . . . immensely readable.'
*The Junior Bookshelf*

*Books by Peter Dickinson:*

The Kin
The Kin: Suth's Story
The Kin: Noli's Story
The Kin: Ko's Story
The Kin: Mana's Story
The Weathermonger
Heartsease
The Devil's Children
Emma Tupper's Diary
The Dancing Bear
The Gift
Chance, Luck and Destiny
The Blue Hawk
Annerton Pit
Hepzibah
Tulku
City of Gold
The Seventh Raven
Healer
Giant Cold
A Box of Nothing
Merlin Dreams
Eva
AK
A Bone from a Dry Sea
Time and the Clock Mice, Etcetera
Shadow of a Hero
Chuck and Danielle
Touch and Go
The Lion Tamer's Daughter

# AK

Peter Dickinson

MACMILLAN CHILDREN'S BOOKS

First published in Great Britain 1990 by Victor Gollancz Ltd

This edition published 2001 by Macmillan Children's Books
a division of Macmillan Publishers Limited
25 Eccleston Place, London SW1W 9NF
Basingstoke and Oxford
www.macmillan.com

Associated companies throughout the world

ISBN 0 330 48204 1

3 5 7 9 8 6 4 2

A CIP catalogue record for this book is available from
the British Library.

Typeset by Intype London Ltd
Printed and bound in Great Britain by Mackays of Chatham plc, Kent

# AK

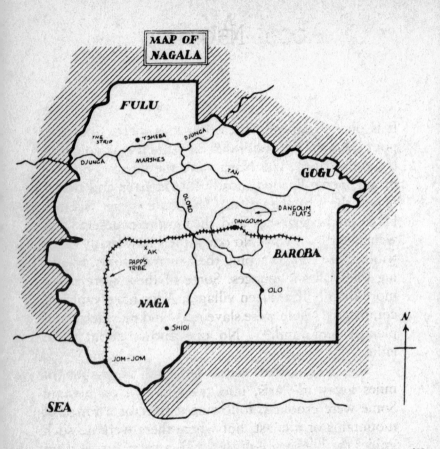

# MAP OF NAGALA

FULU

THE STRIP

TSHEBA

DJUNGA

DJUNGA

MARSHES

TAN

GOGU

OLORO

DANGOUM FLATS

DANGOUM

×AK

PAPP'S TRIBE

BAROBA

OLO

NAGA

SHIDI

JOM-JOM

SEA

N

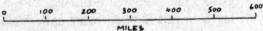

| 0 | 100 | 200 | 300 | 400 | 500 | 600 |

MILES

# About Nagala ...

It is on no map of Africa, but it is there, this vast, poor country. For thousands of years it was no country, only tribes. The Naga were the biggest, but the proud, fierce Baroba mostly fought over and dominated the eastern areas. The Fulu were isolated between the marshes and the northern deserts and went their own way. No one knows how many other tribes there were, keeping their own customs, speaking their own languages. Some of them were never more than half a dozen villages. A lot have vanished completely. There were slave raids and massacres and plagues and famines. No one knows about them either.

Then, a hundred years ago and thousands of miles away in Paris, lines were drawn on a map. Some were crooked, following a river or a range of mountains or a coast, but where there were no such guides the lines were drawn with a ruler. Inside them lay a brand-new country called Nagaland, which the men in Paris had agreed belonged to the British. The British came to Nagaland and stopped the slave raids, and had forced labour instead. They stopped the massacres, and had punitive expeditions with bullets instead of spears. They did their best to stop the plagues and famines, and sometimes succeeded.

They found zinc in the Baroba hills, so they ordered the Baroba to stop being warriors and start being miners. To get the zinc out they built a railway to the coast, across the Dangoum Flats, where no one lived, and they drilled down into the Dangoum aquifer for water for the railway. But they found far more water than they needed, so they decided to build a capital for their new country over the aquifer, so that none of the tribes could say they were favouring any of the others. This must have seemed a good idea to people in London, looking at a map. It was a pity Dangoum turned out a terrible place to live. It still is.

As well as the railway the British built a few roads and schools and hospitals. That is to say they decided how and where to build them and ordered the village headmen to provide forced labour to do the job. It still cost money and Nagaland was a poor country. The zinc was valuable but the mines belonged to Naga Mineral Exploitation, which was a company in London, so very little of the money stayed in Nagaland.

The British ruled for seventy years. Then they worked out how much it was costing them and decided to leave. They explained to the people what a ballot-box was, and a cabinet, and an opposition, and so on. There was a romantic ceremony at which the Union Jack was lowered and the flag of Nagala – as the country was now called – was raised, and democracy began.

Democracy wasn't easy. So many different tribes, so many different ways of life, so many different languages.* And on top of that the British had had a rule that no African could ever be promoted to a position where he might have to give orders to a European, so any ambitious African had chosen to be a doctor, or a lawyer, or a priest. No one had learnt how to run an agricultural improvements scheme, or a road maintenance department, or anything like that. The only place where Africans could really rise had been the army. So it was not at all surprising, first, that the democratic government of Nagala made a real mess of their job, and then that Major Boyo decided to do something about it.

One morning his troops surrounded the Parliament Building and arrested everyone in it. Most of the Cabinet had been tried and shot by nightfall, and the leaders of the Opposition parties next day. Apart from three members of Major Boyo's own small tribe, all the rest simply disappeared. Major Boyo became President Boyo.

Then, hundreds of miles away in the south, beyond Shidi, the war began. A man called Ako Malani led a few others into the bush and started a guerrilla campaign against Boyo's rule. Five years later, when Boyo was assassinated and the neighbouring states forced

* In Nagala anyone who travels much can get along in Naga, and many townspeople and traders speak English, especially for talk between people who have different home languages. Almost all the talk in this book is in Naga, for which I've used ordinary English. I don't want to keep explaining which language is being used, so for English itself I've mostly used a version of the Englishes that are talked in Africa. These are not 'bad' Englishes. They are different forms of the language, with their own rules and grammar. Many of the people who use them can talk ordinary English as well, when it suits them.

the army to accept civilian rule, people imagined the war would end. But the elections were rigged. The new politicians in Dangoum belonged to parties with democratic-sounding names, all with different initials but all much the same, and between them almost as bad as Boyo, in different ways. The army did what it liked, so the war went on. And on. And on.

Until the day on which this story begins.

# One

The day the war ended.

In the dawn of that day Paul lay for a while in a vague world between dream and waking. In his dream there'd been a hut made of grass and mud, a girl chanting at the door as she pounded mealie in the bowl cradled between her knees. He had known her . . . he remembered . . . he tried to hold on to his dream of her . . . she was gone. And the dreamer who had belonged in that world . . . he was gone too.

Automatically he moved his left hand an inch and closed it round the night-chilled metal of his AK. At once the dream-world was forgotten and he knew exactly who he was, Paul, Warrior, of the Fifth Special Commando of the Nagala Liberation Army, now out on a mission to blow up and ambush the Grand Trunk Railway between Dangoum and Jomjom. Who he was, what he was, all he was. Paul. Warrior. A boy with his own gun.

He didn't often need to tell himself this. Usually he knew it even in his sleep, and his dreams were dreams about the war; but once a month or so the dream about the hut came back, disturbing his certainties until the cold touch of the AK banished it. Then he would lie with his eyes shut, telling himself what he knew about his real world, making it come solid again.

It was a small world, the Fifth Commando, a unit

specializing in dangerous raids into government territory. Twenty-three grown men and ten Warriors. Michael was leader and Fodo was second-in-command. The Warriors were boys whom the commando had picked up, one way or another, during the war, and were training to be soldiers. About half the men had been Warriors once. Michael said that they must be called Warriors, not boys, because what they were doing was no business for a child. He gave each new Warrior an Uncle, one of the men to keep an eye on him, teach him the craft of war, protect him if necessary. In return the Warriors did small jobs for their Uncles, made and brought them their meals, washed their clothes, built and fed their fires and so on. Paul felt himself to be particularly lucky because Michael himself was his Uncle.

That was Paul's world. When he had made it fully solid he opened his eyes to begin the day . . .

The men decided that the war was over. The first hint came while Paul was heating Michael's maize-porridge for breakfast. Fodo and Papp were squatting by the radio with Michael, with their blankets wrapped round their shoulders against the chilly bush dawn. Paul knew that what was being said on the radio must be important because Michael had woken the other two up to hear it, though they had come back from reconnoitring the railway line long after midnight, and normally he'd have let them sleep on. Fodo was angry, not because of being woken, but at what he was hearing on the radio. He made sharp grunts of disagreement, like a jackal's bark. Michael ignored him, squatting with his head bowed and scratching with a twig at the yellow earth.

As soon as the voice on the radio stopped, Fodo began to argue. Papp looked puzzled. Michael listened to Fodo, totally still except for the hand where it prodded at the earth with its twig. Paul admired the stillness, which seemed to him full of strength, like a hunting leopard waiting for its moment to pounce, with only the tip of its tail twitching to and fro. Michael said something to Fodo which stopped his grumblings short. The porridge was hot so Paul scooped it on to the platter and passed the pot to Francis so that he could warm Papp's porridge. Michael looked up and smiled, when Paul handed him the platter.

'My thanks,' he said. 'Now go and tell the other Warriors to stop what they're doing and go out and relieve the sentries. I want the sentries back here. You needn't wait to put the fires out. Take water – we may be a long time. I want all ten of you, in pairs. Tell Seme to choose the extra posts himself.'

Paul trotted back for his AK, told Francis what Michael had said and then went and found Seme. The camp was spread out as they were deep into government territory and the bush here was too thin to hide twenty-three men and ten Warriors sleeping in a huddle. All the Warriors were up, heating porridge for their Uncles. This was the only hot meal anyone would have for a long while, as the attack on the railway would keep them on the move till dusk and it wouldn't be safe to light a fire after dark and who knew what might happen tomorrow? Soon the men who hadn't got Warriors to help them would take over the fires to heat their own porridge, but it was usually the Warriors' job to come back and see that the fires were out and the ashes covered.

Seme was leader of the Warriors because he was oldest, about thirteen. Michael said Paul was probably a year younger, but none of the Warriors knew their real ages because they'd all been found wandering in the bush. Some of them could remember the soldiers coming to their villages and burning and shooting, but Paul couldn't, except sometimes in his nightmares. He couldn't even remember his own name – he'd wiped all that out – so Michael had christened him Paul.

Seme frowned when Paul gave him the message and glanced to where his uncle, Judah, was kneeling by a fat-leaved *badi*-bush. Most of Michael's commando were Christian, and Judah had been training to become a priest when the war had sucked him in. He still prayed a lot. Seme didn't want to interrupt him, but orders were orders. He picked up his AK, went over and touched Judah on the shoulder and whispered in his ear. Judah nodded and returned to his prayers. Between them Seme and Paul collected the rest of the Warriors and took them to relieve the sentries.

Michael had been right about the water. The chill and dewy dawn became brilliant day, fresh and tingling with life for a little while as the sun rose but then building to a weight of heat and light that pressed everything down, too dazzling to watch unblinking but despite that dull, weary, endless.

Paul lay hidden under the branches of a fallen but still living thunder-tree, with the foresight of his AK reaching almost to the edge of the twigs. A faint path ran down to the plain which reached away northwards, all the same with its yellow earth and flat-topped trees and tussocks of spiky grey grass, waiting for the rains. Two mole-crickets called from their burrows, one a few yards away and the other further along the slope. Paul could half remember, as part of his dream-life before the war, an old woman telling him why mole-crickets called like that – something to do with the bush-spirit – but Michael had laughed when he'd asked and said that really they were males calling for females to come and mate with them, and the ones who called loudest got the most females. He'd explained how they shaped their burrows like a man cupping his hands round his mouth to shout, so that the calls would carry further. Still, Paul would have liked to know about the bush-spirit too.

Francis was a few yards away, lying in a half-cave under the fallen trunk. The Warriors always watched in pairs. It was good training for the young ones – Francis was only eight – and it was useful if one of them could run back to the camp with a message while the other stayed on watch. Not long after Paul had been found by the commando he had been on sentry with an older Warrior called Didi. Two men had come up the track they were watching, looking like villagers, with leather loin-cloths and a blanket across one shoulder. Paul had been too small then to be allowed a gun but he'd known what to do. He'd scuttled back, got on to the path and walked along it towards the men. The moment he'd rounded the corner that brought him in sight of them he'd stopped, as any child would have done, coming across strangers, with the war crackling to and fro through the bush. Michael said that even a government soldier would hesitate a half-second before shooting a child, so it was a way of finding out what strangers were up to without showing them that there was a commando near by.

The man in front had hesitated for that blink, then had twitched his blanket aside and brought down the gun it had been hiding. But the blink had given Paul time to flick himself sideways and down round the corner with the bullets whipping through the bush above him. They'd stopped, but the batter of gunfire had lasted a couple of seconds longer. Feet flapped away down the path. Paul had lain in the hot silence till he'd heard Didi's soft call, then had risen and peered round the corner. A man was lying by the path with his gun beneath him. The other man was gone.

Didi was dead now, too. Some sort of tick-fever, Judah had guessed, but the men who'd been taking him to hospital had come back saying he'd died before they could get him there. The gun which Paul had pulled from under the man's body was an AK, airborne model with the folding butt. It had seen a lot of service, and had a deep gouge running slantwise across the receiver-cover, but it still worked perfectly well. It lay in front of Paul now. It was his gun.

Towards the middle of the morning a new mole-cricket called, close by, a double chirp which real mole-crickets don't make. Francis had seen something. Paul narrowed his eyes and peered between the twigs, moving his head from side to side to bring fresh reaches of the plain into view. Heat made the distances waver, bounce and fold. A herd of small buck was grazing half a mile away to the right, but they'd been there all morning. Paul had drawn his breath for a call of query when some lens of heated air stretched itself flat for a second or two and there the men were, five of them, moving in line from left to right, further off than the buck. The heat hid them and brought them back, then hid them again. They had the movement of men carrying guns, a sort of confidence you get to recognize, but they were too distant for Paul to see the weapons or whether they were wearing uniform. The one in front looked like a tracker. They might be a government patrol, but they were still several miles from the railway. Much more likely poachers. Paul made a cricket-call, flattening the note at the end to make it say *OK, seen them*. Michael hated poachers. When the commando caught any he took their guns away and told them to clear out, and if he caught them again he'd kill them.

Vanishing and reappearing the men moved across the plain. The sentinel buck saw them and signalled to the rest of the herd. Every animal looked up at the same instant. The herd drifted closer.

Nothing else happened until a little after noon when Paul heard a quiet leopard-cough close behind him. He answered with a cricket-call and Seme crept in under the branches beside him.

'We're to come back to camp.'

'Did you see the poachers?'

'Yes. I told Peter.'

'Who's coming to take over here?'

'They're only setting two sentries, Peter says. He says the war's over.'

'What does that mean?'

'I don't know.'

The camp had changed, its feel as well as its look. The men squatted in groups round the still smouldering fires, arguing aloud. Back at base there might be fierce arguments, about how to fight, and who was winning,

11

and who to trust, and so on. But out on a mission you kept your voice low and you put out fires and you stayed wary and didn't argue because you knew what you were doing and why you were there. And before an action everything became quieter still as the tension grew and grew . . .

But all that was different now. The men were relaxed, some of them cheerful and others angry, as Fodo had been. But they were all uncertain. It wasn't just the camp that had changed, it was the world. The war was over.

Seme gathered the Warriors round the fire Paul had built that morning. The last grey embers had not yet lost the shape of the branches they had once been, so somebody must have been feeding it. Perhaps they'd wanted a second helping of porridge, or perhaps they'd kept the fire going, in spite of the heat, as a way of signalling the change. Tom and Francis fetched food and drink and they all settled in a ring, chewing the salty sun-dried beef-sticks and sipping from the mug as it was passed around. Michael and Fodo joined them and when Michael took the mug he drained it and handed it back to Thomas for a refill. The Warriors stared.

'Only half a day back to the river,' he said. 'Camp there this evening. Have a party.'

He smiled round the circle, forcing the boys to smile back. Some did so without a thought, but Bandu's lips were quivering. This was the first mission he'd been on with his own gun. He was only allowed to set it to single shots because he still wasn't strong enough to hold the aim steady in rapid fire – AKs always tried to squirt themselves away up to the left – but he had five rounds in his magazine and he'd probably been telling himself stories all morning about how he was going to fire each one of them during the attack on the railway, rescuing the rest of the commando from disaster as he did so. No singsong by the river could make up for that.

'He's telling you the war is over,' said Fodo, anger still in his voice.

'Colonel Malani spoke on the radio this morning,' said Michael. 'He has come to terms with the NDR to form a government of national unity.'

Even the Warriors felt the kick of shock. The Nagala Democratic Republicans were supporters of the government. They were the enemy.

'It's a sell-out,' said Fodo.

'Never in life can you achieve every detail of what you desire,' said Michael. 'If the terms are those Malani described we have eighty per cent. How can we ever have a hundred per cent? How can we hold the north without the NDR? We are forced to co-operate, in the end. But da Yabin and Vang and Chichaka are under arrest and warrants are out for the rest of the RKR leaders. Chichaka will be tried for the Ulumi massacre. Other war crimes will be investigated. Those not convicted will go into permanent exile. There will be UN-supervised elections within eight months. Any honestly conducted elections we are certain to win, so this time next year Malani will be President and perhaps Fodo will be Minister of Sport.'

The boys laughed. Fodo didn't.

'The NDR are a bunch of crooks,' he said. 'Half of them are leftovers from Boyo's time. As soon as Malani took Olo they realized they were on the wrong side and switched.'

13

'We know what they are,' said Michael. 'Malani's not a fool.'

'I bet da Yabin thought the same,' said Fodo. 'I say anyone who tried to work with the NDR will either be cheated by them or become like them.'

'Time will tell,' said Michael. 'But how can we know what it will tell without giving it the chance? What is the alternative? Two more years of war? Three? Four? How many lives? How many millions of dollars? Shall we blow up the railway today so that we can go and repair it tomorrow?'

'I've already told you – I accept Colonel Malani's orders. We have got this far by being better disciplined than anyone else, and that is our sole hope. Tell the Warriors what you wish.'

'My thanks,' said Michael.

He paused and looked round the circle, studying the Warriors one by one.

'You have been heroes,' he said. 'All of you, and so were those who are no longer among you – Japhet, and Didi, and the other Paul, and Bayi. I lay it on you to remember their names for ever. It is for you that they died. But there is going to be no more of children dying in this war. I therefore lay it upon you to live. You are very special children, because you hold in your hands – no, you hold in your *minds* the future of this country. Suppose there had never been a war, what would have happened to you? You would have stayed in your villages, working in your father's fields, or herding his cattle, or learning to fish with his nets, and then you would have married and had your own children and taught them what your fathers had taught you. You would have been good men in your villages. Knowing you, I know that that is true.

14

But now you are going to be much more than that. You are going to be good men in your country. I do not know the ways of Almighty God. I don't know why he allows such horrors and terrors as we have seen. But I do know that always, always, he works things so that out of every horror and terror comes something he can be glad of. Let him be glad of you.

'Look what he has done for you already. He has taken you away from your tribes and clans. Now you can think of something bigger than tribes and clans, because he has put you among men who talk and think and live and breathe that thing. That thing is our country, Nagala. Our country and all its varied people, and how one day, one day soon, they will live together in peace and happiness.

'Now, you can't just say "Let there be peace and happiness". It has to be built, by men and women working together. And even when it is built you can't leave it alone. It has to be tended, it has to be fed and repaired and altered to fit with changing times. It's like a railway, an engine on the railway. That doesn't run by itself. It has to be stoked and driven, its track must be kept sound and the signals working and the bridges inspected – all that. This you will do for Nagala. Colonel Malani and Fodo and I and the others who have led the fighting will try and build the new Nagala, and by the time that's done you will be old enough to help run it.'

'I don't want to be an engine-driver,' said Jonathan. 'I want to be an airline pilot.'

'I'll be a tank commander,' said Goyun.

Some of the Warriors laughed. Michael smiled, but shook his head.

15

'We'll need pilots,' he said. 'We may need tank commanders . . .'

'We'll always need an army,' said Fodo.

'Yes,' said Michael. 'A small, well-trained force, and no guns anywhere else. How can you have laws and justice in a country where every peasant has an AK in his thatch, every townsman a couple of grenades buried in his back yard, and their only idea when they aren't given what they want is to go and kill someone for it? But this isn't your problem, Warriors. This is something Fodo and I and the others must find answers to, so that when your turn comes a peasant with a grievance won't reach into the thatch for his AK but will come to you, and you will see that he is given justice, and whether he wins or loses he will accept it. This is what you will be doing to run our railway. I don't mean I want you all to be judges and lawyers. Efficiency is a form of justice. You will be the people who see that Nagala is efficiently run. You will work in the agricultural research programmes. You will plan the roads. You will collect and administer the finances. You will represent Nagala in the United Nations. You will track down and punish fraudulent businessmen. Do you understand?'

Paul saw the others nodding, and nodded with them. They were doing it to please Michael. It was possible, just, to imagine yourself as a grown man sitting at the controls of an airliner (Paul had seen a picture in a magazine) or leading a squadron of tanks bouncing across the bush, but the things Michael had been talking about were too strange for that.

'So first,' he said, 'you must go to school. You must learn to read and write, and speak English, and do

16

mathematics. You must learn the history of your country, and the histories and geographies of other countries, and then science or engineering or medicine or economics, according to your chosen futures. You must . . .'

There was a shout from the men round the radio. Michael rose and they all went over to listen. Colonel Malani's message was rebroadcast, the light voice speaking in short bursts, full of energy, first in English and then in Naga, and then with interpreters translating each section into Baroba and Fulu. Paul tried to follow the Naga, which was the language the commando spoke among themselves. (It wasn't the language he'd spoken as a child – that had been something different, which none of the men had recognized, and now Paul could remember only a few words from a song someone used to sing him to sleep with.) When the commando was resting between operations Joshua ran a school for the Warriors, so they could all write their letters and speak some English, though nothing like enough to follow Colonel Malani's rapid sentences. But even in Naga, though he understood the words, Paul was bewildered by the meanings – the details of the cease-fire, the conditions for the interim government, the integration of liberation forces into a restructured Army of Nagala, surrender of weapons, rehabilitation and resettlement of displaced persons, demilitarization of intertribal zones . . .

His fingers felt their way along the gouge on the receiver-cover of the AK, as if they were caressing the scar of an old wound. No, he wasn't going to be allowed to keep his gun – at least he understood that much. What would become of it? Would they give it

17

to a regular soldier, this old, battered weapon, when there were so many others to choose from? Put it in a store, in case another war started? Sell it in a batch for a few dollars each to someone else in Africa whose war was still going on? Destroy it? That wouldn't be easy. An AK was tough. That was why everyone wanted one, for this kind of war. It mightn't fire as quickly or as accurately as other guns, but long after those others had jammed or malfunctioned it would still be working. Daniel, who'd trained all the Warriors in the use of their weapons, had told them a story about a soldier who'd been wading through a marshy stream somewhere out west and had caught his foot in something buried in the mud. He found that the sling of an AK had tangled itself round his ankle. Somebody must have dropped it during the previous season's campaigning. With the mud and reed-roots still clinging to it he'd cocked it, eased the safety and pulled the trigger. The AK had fired.

Paul liked the story. He could imagine something like that happening with his own gun. He was sure it would fire too. He couldn't bear the idea of it being deliberately destroyed. Hadn't it fought for Nagala every bit as much as he had, every step of the way, three whole years in the bush, at Kumin Bridge, and at Tala, and the ambush at Fos? He'd never killed anyone with it as far as he knew, because mostly the Warriors' fire-power was used to give cover while the men made an attack, and in the last year they'd spent a lot of time guarding prisoners, who'd been only too glad to be captured and weren't interested in running away. Still, it was a good gun, a hero too.

While the translators were speaking the men argued among themselves, and when the broadcast

18

was over the discussions went on. They were still at it when Papp held up his hands and told them to listen. For a while there was nothing but the call of the crickets and the usual bush rustlings and tickings, but then, far off, a slow, wailing hoot, repeated three times. They all knew what it meant. The railway was single-track, with passing-places. The train from the coast was now waiting at one of these, with its guard of government soldiers out round it. There would be more of these than usual because attached to the empty ore-carriages were three trucks of military supplies, including some vital helicopter spares. Papp must have heard it signalling that the line was clear – he came from a real bush tribe and could often hear or somehow sense movements and presences that no one else could. Now, in the silence, they could all hear the triple hoot of the loaded ore-train signalling that it was coming through. War or no war, their long-planned mission to break the line and destroy the military stores had failed.

Now the arguments changed to whether they should head back at once for the river or spend the night here. Soon it was too late not to stay. The Warriors were sent to gather wood. Several men went off to hunt some of the buck Paul had seen, while Papp and Francis looked for other ingredients for a victory feast. Papp could find things to eat in almost-desert. Newcomers to the commando – some of them had never eaten anything except milk and blood-porridge from their cattle – had made faces when they were offered things like termite grubs and thistle ribs, but they'd learnt before long to be glad of them.

A dead thunder-tree lay nearby, so there was more than enough wood. The Warriors piled it up and then settled in a ring, imitating the men, to argue whether Colonel Malani was right to accept the cease-fire, or was it a disastrous mistake, throwing away everything they'd fought for, or was he really only another ambitious soldier, ready to betray his followers as soon as he saw a chance to seize power for himself? Paul didn't want to argue, or listen. The boys understood even less than the men. Michael was leader still. Why couldn't they all go on doing what he told them, the way they had until yesterday?

The shrill voices battled pointlessly to and fro. Paul slipped away and found a patch of shade by a butcherthorn, where he carefully dismantled his AK, oiling each part, the magazine, the receiver-cover, the bolt and bolt-carrier, the return spring, the barrel and body, with all the oil he had left. He plugged both ends of the barrel with a wad of oily rag, then wrapped each part in a piece of plastic maize-bag, tying them round with trip-cord. He made a separate parcel of his eighteen rounds and fitted the whole lot into another bag, which he lashed tight. He took one of the mattocks which the commando carried for mine-laying and walked away from the camp, but once out of sight he circled to the left, so that no one who had noticed him leave would be able to guess where he had finished up.

He chose a place with three good landmarks around it, an oblong boulder, a termite's nest and a bean-tree, and carefully paced out and memorized the distances. The work took him till after dusk. He came back by the same route, switching a branch to and fro behind him to wipe out any footprints.

Dark though it was there was no trouble finding the camp. You could have seen the fire from the railway twelve miles away. He smelt scorching meat. He had heard shots soon after he'd started digging and had stood stock still, every sense sharp with alarm and doubt. Then he'd heard distant cheering and carried on. The war was over indeed.

He slipped into the circle beside Seme as though he'd only been out into the bush for a piss, but Michael must have been watching for him, because in a minute or two he came and squatted by Paul's side, in silence, as if thinking of nothing but his hunger, while the fat of two buck sizzled down into the red embers.

'You were a long time,' he muttered. 'Put it good and deep?'

'Yes. Do you want to see where?'

'That's your secret.'

There was another silence. Paul had believed he'd got his crying done while he was slogging with the mattock at the hard yellow earth. If anyone had found him there they'd have thought the tears were just sweat. Now he felt they'd come again, and he couldn't hide them. He forced himself to stare around. On the far side of the circle reflected firelight glittered from the eyeballs of his friends. Their teeth shone white.

'Said a prayer?' asked Michael.

'My thanks, I said. Hope I'm not needing you again.'

'My prayer too.'

Another silence, their own, private, untouched by chatter and happy mockery round the fire.

'What d'you want to do next?' said Michael.

'School, like you told us, I suppose.'

'And after?'

21

'Don't know.'

'You don't want to be a rock star?'

'No. Not an airline pilot either. I suppose it depends what I turn out any use doing. Only thing I know so far is being a Warrior.'

'Uh. You've been good at that. Too good? That kind of life can take you over.'

'I feel it already. I see it in some of the men.'

'Only some of them.'

Another silence.

'What'll you be doing, Michael?'

Michael laughed and stretched his arms as if he could see his future close in front of him, big and full of action.

'First, get as near as I can to Malani,' he said. 'Promised me good work, soon as the war's over. Of course he's made more promises than he can keep, so maybe I'll be unlucky, but I think he'll reckon I'm one of the ones he can trust, because I don't want as much as some. There'll be some asking to be made generals, and some looking for posts where they can get themselves rich, and three or four waiting for the day when they can push Malani aside and step in his shoes, but me, all I want once we've got things settled is to look after the National Parks.'

'What's a National Park?'

'Big stretch of bush and forest with wild animals in it. Maybe a few bush people. Tourists come to see it and photograph the animals and so on, so it brings cash into the country. We've got to have at least one. But you can't just point at a map and say, "This area's a National Park from now on." There's work to do, stopping poaching, keeping the farmers out, providing facilities for the tourists, managing the animals.

Amazing what a mess you get soon as there's a few too many elephant in one place . . .'

He laughed again, happy with the thought of his dream, seen so clear for the moment through the glow of the fire.

'I'll come and help with the poachers,' said Paul.

'Maybe. But school first.'

'You'll be around?'

'Don't know. I'll come and see you whenever I can, though. I'm not leaving you on your own, Paul. I've been calling myself your uncle because that's how we decided to do it in this commando, in case some of the boys might find their real fathers again one day. I don't see how that can happen for you, so from now on I'm your father and you're my son. Maybe I'll marry and have children of my own, but whatever happens you'll be my eldest son. All right?'

Paul felt for Michael's hand and held it. A thought struck him.

'Your wife mightn't like it.'

Michael's laugh this time was loud enough to break the bubble of privacy around them. Warriors and men to either side stopped their talk for a moment to glance across.

'I'll tell her she's my second wife,' he said. 'My first wife was the war. She was a cruel bitch but she gave me a son, and then she went and died. Good riddance.'

Paul laughed too, but afterwards, while he chewed at the sweet tough meat and the juices ran down his chin, he decided it might be more than a joke. My mother was the war, he thought. She was a witch, a terrible demon, an eater of people, but she looked after me. It's not my fault that I loved her.

23

# Two

The first school was the one back at base camp, bare earth under palm trees till the rains came – heavy that year – and then an open-sided tent, with the boys hunched over their slates in the listless sticky air. The school grew as other commandos came out of the bush. Two real school huts came in trucks from the coast and were assembled in a day, and a Swedish pastor from the churches which had given the huts blessed them, while Colonel Malani himself flew in from Dangoum to perform the opening ceremony. The whole camp paraded for him, the men still carrying their guns, but the two hundred and eleven boys and thirty-five girls marching past with their slates. Colonel Malani said that these were the weapons of the future. Later Michael told Paul that he himself had written that bit into the speech. He'd stood next but one to the Colonel on the saluting base and ridden in his Land Rover on his tour of the camp.

Michael was working eighteen hours a day. He headed the bureau for the resettlement of troops who were not being integrated into the regular army; he was on the commission to draw up the new constitution; he was on the liaison committee for the distribution of aid funds which were pouring into the country because the rich nations were so happy about the war ending, or pretended they were. Trouble with Michael, Judah said, was that you could trust him, so he got landed with the jobs where trust was important. Even so he managed to come out to the camp at least once a week on resettlement business, and saw Paul then.

When the rains ended the camp started to break up, and the Warriors were sent to new schools in their own tribal homelands, where these were known. Michael came out specially to talk to Paul about his future. He picked him up in his own Land Rover, with a uniformed driver and a uniformed guard in the back seat. Both carried AKs. As soon as they were out of sight of the camp the Land Rover stopped, the driver moved to the back seat and Michael drove on out into the bush. He stopped on the crest of a low hill, right up on the skyline, a target for miles. That didn't matter any more.

The soldiers stayed in the car and smoked and listened to Radio Dangoum while Michael spread a picnic out on a flat-topped rock. They ate with their legs dangling over its edge, looking north-east across the Oloro valley with its belt of lush green forest to the bush country beyond, green too after the rains, but by next month back into its dry-season colour, the colour of lions. Michael ate only a few mouthfuls, then lit a thin cigar and smoked, gazing out over the valley.

'So short a season,' he said. 'In Europe it's green nine months of the year. A lot of the fields are green all winter.'

'But the snow is white?' said Paul. 'Really white?'

'Didn't snow at all the winter I was there. You want snow you've got to go to Switzerland.'

'Switzerland where the money's going?' said Paul.

'What money? Who told you that?'

'Just joking in the camp. About we get up the taxes and pass the money to the NDR so they can send it to Switzerland.'

'Not true,' said Michael.

He stubbed out his hardly-smoked cigar and tossed it down the slope.

'Next time you hear this,' he said, 'tell them it's not true. Tell them from me, Michael Kagomi.'

'I can tell them the NDR are OK?'

'Didn't say that. Just we're getting them tied so they can't get their hands in the mealie-bag, the way da Yabin let them. Who's been starting these stories, d'you know?'

'Just talk. Comes from nowhere. Like water in the river.'

'River comes from somewhere. How many left in your school now? It was getting on two-fifty when Malani came.'

'Bit under a hundred left, maybe.'

'What did you make of them? Get on with them all all right? Some of them had had a really rough time, you know.'

'There's a few of them act like they were dreaming – bad dreams, like I used to get, only they've got them all the time. They're in a special class and there's a nun who tries to help them. There's some just had it tough. I've got a friend – his name's Quaab – his commando wasn't like ours, more like government soldiers. If the men found women or girls in the bush they'd rape them soon as look at them, and then just leave them. If they couldn't get women they took the Warriors to bed with them. I didn't guess how lucky I'd been, finding you, till I talked with Quaab.'

Michael nodded and sat silent.

'There's another lot, call themselves the Leopards,' said Paul. 'They act like the war wasn't ended. They come marching into class like as if they were on drill parade. I tried to get talking with one of them once when I got him alone – mostly they go around three or four together. I got a feeling he'd like to talk, but he didn't. Made no difference – next day he'd been knocked about. None of them said anything to me. Just looked.'

'What do they say in political classes? You have political classes?'

'Mondays and Thursdays. They don't say a thing, just sit yawning. They're all Baroba, and they talk Baroba among themselves, but it isn't just that.'

Michael took out another cigar, lit it and drew silently on the smoke. Just another change from the war, when three men would share a cigarette, stubbing it out between puffs so that it would last longer. Cigarettes were still short in the camp, but Michael seemed to have cigars to throw away.

'Yeah,' he said. 'You get that after a revolution. These kids are just copying their men. There were some real hard-line Maoist groups up among the zinc mines. Now they think whatever settlement we've got isn't enough and they want to go on fighting. Let them have their way and you've got Cambodia.'

Paul didn't know about Cambodia, so he just nodded. Michael took a pad out of his pocket and made some notes.

'They'll have seen you come out with me,' he said. 'Maybe you'd best keep clear of them till I've got you shifted – that's what I've come to talk to you about.'

'Provided it's near you.'

Michael shook his head.

'I'll be mostly stuck in Dangoum,' he said.

'Aren't there any schools there?'

'Sure, but it's not where I want you. Two reasons. For a start you'd hate it. Dangoum's got everything wrong a city can have wrong, flat and hot and stinking. Right in the middle there's the stupid great palace Boyo had built for himself, and round that there's a few decent buildings, modern high-rises, and round that there's what's left of the town the British built, all tatty and broken up, and round that there's the shanties. You should see the shanties. It's happening all over Africa. You get farmers on the land but there's never enough land and anyway the living's dirt poor, so they head for the city looking for a better living. Of course they don't find it, but they don't go back home and new ones don't stop coming, so the city grows and grows till it's millions of poor people with nothing to live on. Then the government has to keep food prices down to stop the riots, and to do that they squeeze the farmers, so the farmers can't make a living and decide to head off for the cities, and meanwhile the economy gets shot to hell and the foreign debts go up and up . . . at least in Dangoum we've got the Flats to make getting there difficult, but people are still coming across somehow. We've got to stop it. And for that we've got to set an example, not fetching our own families in all the time.'

'And I'm your family.'

'That's right, and I'm going to do the best I can for you. That's the second reason. We're planning to start some special schools for the most promising kids, and we're deliberately not putting them in Dangoum. We're spreading them round the country. Where do you think your home is, Paul?'

28

'I don't know. Wherever you live, I suppose.'

'An eighth storey apartment in a Dangoum high-rise?'

'Then my home is the bush.'

'That's over. What I'm trying to tell you is you haven't got a home yet, though you will have one one day. But for the moment I'm not doing you any wrong if I ask you to go to school at Tsheba, up beyond the marsh country.'

'In Fulu!'

'And while you are there you will learn Fulu, and how the Fulu live and what their needs and hopes are, and Fulu children will go south into Naga and east into Baroba and learn about them. And at the same time the people of these countries will feel that they can trust the other tribes, because the other tribes are trusting them with their children . . .'

'I'm going to be a kind of hostage?'

Michael sighed.

'If things go very badly it may come to that,' he said. 'Tsheba will be a good school, Paul. An Italian aid group is paying for the buildings. There will be good teachers . . . You know, I'm beginning to think it was a mistake at Independence calling this country Nagala. We should have given the others a look-in.'

'There's a lot more of us Nagai.'

'You're not Naga, Paul.'

'Don't know about my own people. I'm your son now.'

'Well, I'm not Naga either. I'm Nagala. Anyway, I'm asking you if you will go and get your schooling in Tsheba, among the Fulu.'

'Will I know anyone there?'

'There'll be some from the camp school, certainly. From our own commando just you and Francis.'

'Is Papp in the government too?'

Paul was surprised. Papp had been Francis's uncle, but he'd never been interested in politics. He was important in the commando because he was the best tracker and really understood the bush, but he was fighting because government troops had cut down the tree where the ghosts of his ancestors nested in the form of weaver-birds, and when the clan had tried to stop it the soldiers had murdered them.

'Papp's gone back to the bush,' said Michael. 'He'll be useful there, for explaining things to his people. But Francis is a very bright boy, which is why we want him at Tsheba. If things go right for him he will be Prime Minister one day. The Right Honourable Dr Francis Papp, Prime Minister of Nagala.'

Paul laughed aloud at the picture of little Francis, with his round still baby-like face, standing among his grown-up ministers and telling them what to do. Michael laughed too.

'If you were my actual son,' he said, 'I would simply tell you to go to Tsheba, whatever you thought yourself. As it is I can only ask you. You must choose.'

Paul didn't hesitate.

'My name is Paul Kagomi,' he said. 'I *am* your son. I will go to Tsheba.'

The school looked southward over the marshes. Behind it, to the north, lay hundreds of miles of stony desert. Sister Mercy had a photograph of the desert in flower, sheets of garish pink and yellow and purple, but that only happened about once in seven years when a rain-belt went off course and strayed up from the south-west. Then the desert plants would grow and flower and set seed inside six weeks, and the seeds would bury themselves among the scorching pebbles and wait for the next chance rains. At other seasons not even Papp could have lived more than a few days there.

In front of the school, eight miles away, lay the great marsh basin. The Oloro flowed into it from the south and the Tan and the Djunga from the east, and there their waters lay and mingled and steamed among the reed-beds and then somehow, imperceptibly, found their way west and became a river again, still called the Djunga, which flowed towards the ocean. At its point of outflow it was half the size of any of the three rivers where they flowed in. All the rest of the water, eighty-five per cent of it Sister Mercy said, had gone up in steam.

There was a picture of how the school would look when the Italians had finished building it, like a low, sparkling white cliff with sheets of glass beneath its overhangs, just below the ridge of the gentle slope of hills with which the desert ended. Meanwhile the children lived and were taught in tents again. But now they had proper exercise books, and printed books to read from, and calculators and geometry kits and a microscope, and two battery-powered computers (which didn't like the humid heat from the marshes so only worked some of the time).

Paul was not completely pleased to find that little Francis had been promoted into his class after the first two weeks and was sitting beside him. It took him another few days to realize he was lucky Francis hadn't been sent on still higher. Francis didn't seem to find anything difficult, and loved the school-work, partly because he was so good at it but partly, Paul guessed, because filling his mind with it helped him forget the horrors he'd seen. (Unlike Paul he seemed to remember things right back to when he was almost a baby.) He missed Papp, too. Some of the other boys resented knowing that someone so young was cleverer than they were, and said cruel and stupid things to him. Paul found him crying one day and tried to cheer him up by telling him what Michael had said.

'If you're going to be Prime Minister,' he said, 'you'll need a bodyguard. I'll do that.'

'My thanks,' said Francis, totally serious.

'I'm not going to do it for ever, mind,' said Paul. 'When I stop school I'm going to be a game warden in a National Park.'

About half the children were Nagai, a third Baroba and the rest from other tribes, except Fulu. They all learnt English, and the three main languages, which they were supposed to practise on each other, but because there were no Fulu in the school a bus took them down twice a week to the Strip, so that they could team up with Fulu children and practise there.

The Fulu Strip. This was the name the English had given the belt of rich land between the marshes and the hills. To Paul it was the most extraordinary place he had seen. So many people! Such cramped, reeking, bellowing, busy, secret lives! Such work! Paul used to think that the camps were crowded, after the stealth and emptiness of life in the bush, but they were nothing compared with the Strip. When he'd seen pictures of New York or London or Tokyo in magazines he'd tried to imagine himself living in a big, rich city, but in its own way the Strip seemed stranger. Maps marked the Fulu territory as reaching back into the desert, and right across the marshes, and down into the jungly country to the west, but more than nine tenths of the Fulu lived along the Strip.

Near Tsheba it was only a few miles across, but east and west it widened into a plain, patterned green or yellow or almost black according to whether the crops were growing or ripe, or the soil had just been dug and sown for yet another crop in the tiny, crazy-shaped fields. The land was too precious to build on, so the Fulu houses with their round sharp-pointed reed roofs fringed the Strip on both sides, some along the lowest slopes of the hills but many more on stilts in the water.

At dawn the Fulu left their houses. The children herded the buffalo into the marshes while the adults worked in the fields through the day-long, reeking, fly-buzzing haze. The Fulu boast that they are the best farmers in Africa. They need to be. Jilli's family, where Paul and Francis went to practise Fulu, owned shares of five separate fields. In a normal year a field would grow three crops, but they took turns with their co-sharers, which meant they were entitled to seven crops in all. They needed between five and six to live on, so if no crop failed they had food to sell. If one failed they were all right. If two failed they were a bit hungry. If three failed they began to starve.

Jilli was a girl, a bit younger than Paul. Like all the Fulu she seemed from a distance to be a strange, pale, yellowy grey, but meeting her close you saw that this was because her whole body was smeared with a fine clay paste. She wore no clothes except for a grass belt with an apron of blue and white beads. Every fifth day her mother washed and scraped all the old paste

33

off and put on a fresh layer next day. Between past-
ings she had to stay indoors or wear a special red
blanket wrapped round so that only her eyes showed.
If a man were to see her body without its paste either
she'd have to marry him or else her father would have
to pay him to set her free. Sister Mercy said that the
Fulu did get malaria, but not as badly as most people.
Living so close to the marshes for generations they'd
built up immunities, but the clay was supposed to
help too. (Paul and the others were made to smear
themselves with mosquito-repellent before they went
down to the Strip.)

Jilli's father saw no reason why his daughter should
speak anything but Fulu, so the school paid him to let
her stay at home and talk to the boys. Jilli herself,
without telling her father, wanted to learn both Naga
and English, so that in two years' time, just before he
was due to choose a husband for her, she could run
away and become a waitress at the Dangoum Hilton.
So mostly they talked Naga, sometimes guiltily slipping back to English. Francis had actually wanted to
learnt Fulu, but Paul and Kashka had overruled him.
Fulu was much too difficult, all coolings and twitter-
ings. At least Naga and Baroba had the same shape of
sentences and a lot of the same-sounding words.

Kashka was the other member of the team. He was
Baroba, and back at camp he'd been one of the
Leopards, but separated from the others he was
forced to be a bit more friendly. He was two years
older than Paul, with the very black skin-colour and
narrow face most Baroba seemed to have. He never
smiled.

Kashka already knew enough Naga to get by, and
he wouldn't have taught the other two Baroba if

Francis hadn't insisted and got Paul to back him, but that was up at the school. On Fulu mornings the bus would drop them by the roadside and they'd file along a path by an irrigation ditch to Jilli's part of the straggling village, and then across a creaking gangway over the black marsh mud to the first house. The houses were mostly empty now, with everyone out in the fields or the marshes, but if there was anyone at home they would call out, and Francis would answer with the proper Fulu greeting and the person inside would call back giving the boys permission to use the narrow walkway which ran round the edge of each house to the next gangway. Jilli's house stood right out over the water. They'd find the old blind grandmother sitting in the doorway and Francis would greet her and she'd reply, and then Jilli would come smiling out and lead them with her long-legged strut round to the platform on the far side of the house, where they'd sit all morning practising their English and looking out over the steamy marshes.

Behind them the endless noise of the Strip flowed on, the wheeze and clack of bucket-wheels lifting water from the ditches, the flop flop of winnowing, the slower thud of corn being pounded down to meal, the cries of ploughmen to their buffalo teams and the lilt of other voices calling the news and gossip from field to field. The Fulu didn't need to shout. They used a kind of yodelling note which carried a long way. Dr Gonzales, who organized the language rota, said that a really juicy piece of news would get from one end of the Strip to the other, eighty miles away, in less than a morning.

For Paul's last birthday Michael had given him a radio. (It wasn't his real birthday – nobody knew when that was – but the anniversary of that day when a small boy, starving, wild as a jackal, had been caught stealing some of Michael's porridge-meal while he slept.)

'Listen to the BBC World Service,' he'd said. 'Here, or if the signal's bad try here. I'll send you the times of the English lessons, but you listen to anything else you can find.'

Paul took the radio to Jilli's house for their visits, and during the English-by-radio programmes they'd mouth the sentences together. Sometimes they'd get the World News, and understand bits of it. Francis would have listened to anything – science, medicine, arts programmes, politics – even when the names and places meant nothing to him. He had only to hear a word once and he could use it.

'I wish to speak real English,' he said in his slow, childish voice. 'I will speak the way Sister Mary speaks, and Sister Mercy, and Dr Jones.'

'Then you becoming just only black Englishman,' Kashka said. 'When I speaking English, I be making it for me. African.'

'I be speaking both ways,' Paul said.

'I will speak it both ways,' Francis corrected him.

'All you Naga wanting be black Englishmen,' Kashka said.

'I be Nagala, not Naga,' Paul said.

Kashka snorted his scorn. Jilli yawned. She was always trying to tune around for rock programmes. Paul didn't enjoy arguing with Kashka about politics, because Kashka had all his ideas fixed and set, and wouldn't even listen to anyone else's arguments, so he changed the subject. Jilli's grandmother had come round to the platform that morning and was sitting with them working at her endless task of teasing the fibres out of lengths of dried reed so that Jilli's mother and aunts could weave them into mats.

'Don't she hear you not speaking Fulu?' he said. 'Don't she go tell you father you learning English?'

Jilli reached up and caressed the old woman's cheek with her long fingers.

'She too much friend for me,' she said.

She twittered a snatch of Fulu, and the grandmother raised her creased, sunken-cheeked face and answered, proud as a leopard.

'Mans stupid, she saying,' said Jilli.

'Men are stupid,' said Francis automatically. Jilli ignored him. Because they usually spoke Naga she was learning that faster than English, but even in English she was much more confident than Paul had been, shoving the words together any way that suited her and using her spidery hands and mobile face to put the meaning across.

'Mans all stupid,' she said. 'She father, me father, all stupid. Long back she father giving she to stupid man. Now me father doing same. Womans be like buffalo, like basket, uh? She saying no. I saying no. She telling me for to go to Dangoum.'

She jumped up as if she was ready to set out that instant, but only swarmed down the ladder to the boats below and brought up a bundle of fresh-cut reeds, which she spread against the wall of the house to dry. When Paul tried to help her she slapped his hand away.

'Woman work,' she said.

'Women's work,' said Francis.

This time Jilli repeated the words correctly, teasing him by copying his voice. She could if she wanted.

When they let her retune the radio she copied the disc-jockeys.

Twice Jilli took them out into the marshes with messages for her brothers. Like everything else in Fulu the boats were made of reeds, lashed in tight bundles and shaped like stubby canoes. They sat low in the water and were heavy to paddle. The four of them knelt two a side, driving the boat forward, chanting to keep time with their strokes. One of the boats had an outboard motor, but Jilli was never allowed to use it.

Language mornings apart, the school at Tsheba stayed very like the one back at base camp. They were still in tents. The workmen building the new school sometimes didn't turn up for days on end, or when they did they sat around waiting for materials to be delivered. Paul found the work difficult. It didn't take him long to find out that it wasn't only Francis who was cleverer than he was – practically everyone else was, too. They had been picked to go to Tsheba for their brains. But it wasn't just that that set him apart. Though many of the others were orphans, or the children of parents who'd fled for their lives from their villages when the soldiers had come burning and murdering and looting, almost all of them had found their way to refugee camps over one of the borders, where they'd been able to wait till the war was over. Paul and Francis and Kashka were exceptions in their class, because they'd actually fought in the war, lived the life of a Warrior, known that kind of tension, that kind of horror and triumph. It set them apart. Though there were Nagai in the class whom Paul did make friends with, he still found himself easiest in

Kashka's company, despite Kashka's arrogance. Kashka seemed to feel the same, though he would never have admitted it, perhaps not even to himself. They were the ones who understood what it had been like. Francis didn't count. He was too young.

In a way, though Paul had nowhere which he could think of as home, he was homesick. Homesick for the war. He begged a big map of Nagala off Sister Mercy and spent hours trying to work out and mark on it the movements of Michael's commando. There were expeditions of which he felt he could recall every march, every camp site. Sometimes the places were named on the map, or at least marked, a bridge they'd mined, a garrisoned town they'd needed to by-pass, a watering-place where he'd gone alone and naked to count the government trucks and listen for news. Using these and his memories he found that there were areas he'd crossed and re-crossed, so that now if you'd dropped him there by parachute in the dark he could have waited for dawn and looked around and known where he was.

He showed Michael the map when he came up to collect Paul for the Independence Day holidays. Michael laughed but shook his head.

'That's all over,' he said. 'When we've got the present and future shaped up there'll be time for the past.'

'The war was my mother,' said Paul. 'I'm laying her to rest.'

This time Michael checked his laugh and studied the map, tracing the journeys route by route with his forefinger.

'Pretty good,' he said. 'Don't think I could have done that. Something wrong here – the eighty-seven rains we were in Shidi – that's where Papp came to us.

His tribal grounds are over here, either side of the railway just beyond where it turns south. I thought we might fly out there next week and see how he's getting on, and photograph a bit of wildlife.'

'That would be great.'

'I've managed to clear four days. I was hoping for more, but we've got the heads of the Organization of African Unity coming to Dangoum the month after next, and that means a load of extra work for me. I'm afraid you're going to be pretty much on your own in Dangoum till we get away.'

'I shan't mind.'

'Wait and see.'

They drove off in a long black Mercedes with polarized windows, like sunglasses, so that you could see out but not in. The doors closed with a heavy clunk, like the breach of a field-gun.

'Bullet-proof,' said Michael. 'The floor's armoured too, in case of mines. It's one of Boyo's toys – we found five of them in the Palace.'

While he read papers from his briefcase Paul played with the switches and fittings, the drinks cabinet with its silver goblets, the air-conditioner, the TV with no signals to receive, the gun compartment. The car swished westward along a smooth new road which da Yabin's government had built as a show piece, with the Strip and the marshes on their right. After more than an hour they turned south. Soldiers manned a road-block on the causeway over the tongue of marsh where the Djunga funnelled in, but they waved the Mercedes through. On either side of the road-block the ordinary travellers waited, a few old trucks, oxen with panniers, farmers and traders

40

with shoulder-loads and so on. They stared dully at the long black government car. Michael looked up from his work and sighed.

'I never imagined this,' he said. 'How much do you think the soldiers are demanding to let them through? As far as these people can see we are just a continuation of the old oppression, with new initials.'

'Can't you stop the soldiers taking bribes?'

'How? Who will give the orders? Their captain is lining his pockets, and so is his colonel, and so is their general. Do you know what our Minister of Commerce gave his son for his eighteenth birthday? A private helicopter.'

'Wow!'

'One of the many things I've learnt is that governments have extraordinarily little power to make people happy, though they have plenty of power to make them miserable. The people must will their own happiness, the means as well as the end. Nothing else is any use.'

'It'll be all right one day.'

'May you live to see it.'

The miles wore on. There was another road-block at the bridge over the Tan and two more before Dangoum. They drove through bush, between dry eroded hills, past villages with their patches of brown gardens around them. It was nearly dusk when the road entered an endless, pale, dusty plain, almost pure desert. The setting sun wobbled and stretched in the waves of heated air that rose from its barren reaches.

'Dangoum Flats,' said Michael. 'Take a good long look. This is why we had to come to terms with the

NDR, whatever the hot-heads said. Dangoum's a fortress because of the Flats. They're better than trenches and minefields. Give the government in Dangoum a few aeroplanes, a few tanks and armoured cars, and they can hold out against commandos as long as the water in the aquifer holds out, and that means for ever.'

'You said people were still getting across to join the shanties.'

'Mostly in trucks, bribing their way past the roadblocks. Some of them on the railway. Quite a few on foot – there's guides who bring them through, walking at night, though there's some never make it.'

'They're that desperate to get through?'

'They think they are, but when they get there . . . You'd better see for yourself. I'll get Peter to take you into the shanties. The only other things worth seeing in Dangoum are Boyo's palace and the market.'

'Who's Peter?'

'Cooks and cleans my apartment.'

'I could do that.'

'Not your job any more.'

Michael returned to his papers. Paul sat silent, watching the sun sink over the dreadful desert. He was cross with himself for feeling jealous that somebody else should be looking after Michael. He'd much rather have been doing that than going back to school in nine days' time.

# Three

Dangoum was a glow in the dark ahead. Then it was a smell, a sour mixed reek of fumes and dung and rotting food. Then it was a wide double road lined on either side with palms, the grey trunks blip-blip-blipping past in the headlights, with scattered vague lights beyond. Then there were dim wide-spaced street lights with two- and three-storey flat-roofed buildings behind the palms, their walls plastered with peeling posters, and food-stalls lit by glaring butane lamps, and the blare and flicker of a disco. Then tall glass-faced buildings and lit shop-windows and neon signs. And then at the very top of the avenue, so different that it made Paul's mouth open in a silent gasp, the palace Boyo had built, a long white floodlit building with a tower at the centre standing on a low mound, with fountains playing and a ring of water below reflecting the gleam and glitter above.

'Wow!' said Paul.

'American architect,' said Michael. 'Apart from the water-tower it's a copy of some palace in Europe. The fountains look like a waste but water's the one thing Dangoum's got plenty of. The floodlighting is a waste, but we run it for a couple of hours each evening as a way of telling everyone that the war's really over.'

'Is it?'

'Ask me in ten weeks' time.'

'What do you mean?'

Michael shook his head.

The car half-circled the palace, turned down another wide avenue and drew up in front of one of the tall buildings. There was a soldier on guard, who saluted Michael, and a porter who came to carry Paul's case. They rode a lift up.

'Strange feeling, uh?' said Michael.

Paul nodded, determined not to show his sense of wonder. A lift, he told himself, was no more amazing than his AK had been, once you understood it. Just a machine for doing a job.

'When you say your prayers ask for there not to be power cuts. A hundred and eighty-six stairs to climb. Makes a change from Tsheba. I'll show you how the toilet works, and then we'll see what Peter's giving us for supper.'

The windows of the flat looked eastwards. A hundred miles away in the clear morning air Paul could see the blue Baroba hills, beyond the pale Flats and the browner bush. Inside the Flats was a ring of green, fields and gardens irrigated from the aquifer to feed Dangoum, and inside that the fuzz of the shanties, and then, almost at his feet, it seemed, the pattern of the rectangular roofs of the old town, bright-speckled with awnings for people to sleep under during the hot nights and the still hotter noons.

Michael had gone to work before Paul was up, but had left a map of the city and a note saying 'Go and see Boyo's palace this morning. I'll be back about twelve.' The map showed that Dangoum had been planned (by the British, Paul learnt later) as a series of rings round the central mound on which the palace now stood. Twelve wide roads radiated from there, linked to each other at intervals by smaller circling roads. The plan had never been completed and the pattern kept breaking down, but most of the main avenues ran true towards the weird white building at the centre. Paul went up there after breakfast.

The palace was now being run as a tourist attraction, but there were no tourists apart from Paul and a Danish woman journalist who took a lot of photographs and asked even more questions. The guide, a pale-skinned tall thin woman, just smiled and went on with her spiel. She showed them Boyo's state bed, and his fifty-two uniforms, and the shelf after shelf of clockwork toys he'd collected, and the cupboard after cupboard of Paris clothes he'd imported for his wives, and the banqueting hall with the sandbagged section opposite Boyo's chair, so that after dinner he could loll and sip his brandy and see how close he could shoot to one of the prisoners brought up from the cells below. The guide smiled about this too. Paul thought she must be Fulu. She spoke good English but there was a sort of twitter behind it, just like Jilli's. She was still smiling when she took the visitors down to the pumping hall.

This was a wide, dim tunnel running beneath the palace and filled with a steady pulsing, like a double heartbeat. All down the centre water ran in a rushing channel until it reached a black pool, on either side of which the brass pistons of the pump rose and fell. These weren't the main pumps, the guide explained. These only forced the water from the pool up into a huge tank at the top of the tower, from which it then flowed out to feed Dangoum. The pumps that brought the water up from the aquifer itself were another sixty metres underground. The pumping hall and the water-tower had been built by the British, and Boyo had added the rest of his palace round them.

When the guide had finished explaining this she led them to the other end of the tunnel, where the space on either side of the rushing stream had been narrowed to a walkway, with a series of barred doors facing each other across the gap.

'These too Boyo had built,' said the guide. 'They were for his special prisoners. Listen.'

She clicked a switch and a tape started to play, a man's voice explaining how he'd been brought to the pumping hall, and what had been done to him by the guards while he was there, but he'd barely begun on the real horrors when the lights went out and the tape moaned into silence.

'Only a power cut,' said the guide's bubbling voice. 'Please stay still, in case you fall in the water. The power will soon be restored. The palace has its own generators.'

They stood in the haunted dark, listening to the thud of the pumps and the whisper of the stream. Paul tried to imagine what had happened in this place. It was as bad as anything he'd seen in the war. Worse.

A cigarette lighter snapped and the Danish woman's face showed beaky and pale in its glow. She lit cigarettes for herself and the guide.

'And the cells haven't been used since Boyo's time?' she asked.

'It was all closed. The exhibition was not completed.'

'For five years? According to Amnesty International Colonel Chichaka . . .'

'The case of Colonel Chichaka is *sub judice*. Look, here are the lights.'

The lamps barely shone, dim yellow between the cells. There wasn't enough power to drive the tape so the guide switched it off and led the way out, talking as she did so – things she'd already said – to stop the Danish woman asking any more about Amnesty. They came up into daylight at the other end of the palace, in the Hall of the Future, which turned out to be an unfinished exhibition of what the Malani government was going to do for Nagala, with model peasants digging model wells and raising model crops in model fields and working a model cotton-mill. The model game reserve was still being built. New though it all was, the future smelt dull and dusty.

Paul found Michael already in the flat, reading yet more papers and making notes in the margins. Lunch was brought in by Peter, a wrinkled, grinning man, barely taller than Paul. It was maize salad and a little salt beef, nothing special.

'Nowadays Africans all want bread,' said Michael. 'You can't grow wheat here and you can't make bread from maize, so you have to buy it in from Europe or America. If there isn't bread, there'll be riots. What did you make of the palace?'

'Was he mad?'

Michael shrugged.

'Is it mad to want power?' he said. 'Then I am mad too. Almost all men want power. I don't know about women. But if you have power you need to express it, or it ceases to be power. You do this by conquering more and more nations to add to your power, or by building a useless city in the middle of a desert, or by persuading your people to live in peace and happiness, or by shooting a line of bullet holes round a terrified prisoner. In the old days there were kings who ate men's hearts because they believed it added to the power of their own souls. Really it's all the same.'

'And Chichaka used the cells too?'

'Sometimes. It depended how his power struggle with da Yabin was going.'

'I don't understand.'

'May you not. About this afternoon – everyone in Dangoum goes to sleep for two or three hours in the heat of the day. You don't have to do that here, provided the air-conditioner doesn't pack up, so I've got you some rock videos to look at. Then about four you could go out and look around. I'll be back around seven – what would you like to do then?'

'Can we go to the Hilton?'

'If you want. Why?'

Paul explained about Jilli. Michael laughed aloud, the way he sometimes used to in the bush.

'Half the girls in Nagala are after her job,' he said. 'Tell her she'll be much better off learning to type. A good secretary can earn as much as a cabinet minister in this crazy place. Then tomorrow morning Peter can take you down to the market when he goes shopping. I'll give you some gura to spend, and I'll tell him to do a side-trip into the shanties.'

The videos passed the afternoon, slowly. Paul raided the refrigerator again and again, till he had drunk so much Coke he thought he would burst with bubbles. That you should somehow get cold out of heat, this heat – the kitchen wasn't air-conditioned – was more magical than any lift or gun. Later he went out and strolled down through the old town. The air was full of town-smells, the streets just coming to life after the midday rest. Heat still lay on everything, weary and dusty, but laughter and argument rose from the dark innards of the houses, the bars were coming to life, snacks sizzling on the food-stalls down the avenues. Paul watched a couple of police stroll up to one of these and chat affably with the food-seller, who smiled and twinkled and nodded to them while she shaped a couple of paper bowls with deft fingers and ladled in rice and curry. They clapped her on the back like old friends and took the food without paying. The moment their backs were turned her smiles became angry mutters.

That evening the dinner at the Hilton was more than Paul could eat, and more delicious than he could have imagined. The waitresses were all quite as pretty as Jilli. The head waiter, who'd hovered and smiled all through the meal, was startled and a bit affronted when Michael insisted on paying. He was used to important government officials wanting to be fed for nothing. Michael sighed when Paul told him about the policeman at the food stall.

'You can change the laws,' he said. 'That's easy. But how can you change whole ways of life? You were right about Switzerland, by the way.'

There'd always been a market in Dangoum, Michael said. Even before the British had built the town there'd been two or three stalls there, selling salt from the Flats and the dried bodies of yellow lizards to be used in anti-witch charms, and things like that. The aquifer had been just a conical hole in the ground then, with a muddy pool at the bottom, but it was the only water in the Flats so two trade routes had crossed there.

Now a blind man using his ears could have found the market from a mile away. The noise was as loud as a battle. Most of it came from an enormous sound system, loud-speakers hoisted on to the trunks of a group of old palms near the centre and belting out music full volume all day long. An old man with no legs sat beneath the trees to change the tapes. He was stone deaf from the drumbeat. Round the palms was a wide space, several hundred yards square, filled with stalls. Some of them had their own sound systems, playing different music. Others simply added to the noise with the shouts of the traders and the cackle and bray of animals. Doctors thrust bottles of coloured stuff under the noses of passers-by and bellowed about cures. Beggars wailed prayers. Over in the metalsmiths' section the clatter of hammers was loud enough to drown the music from the main speakers – the noise was a sort of element, like air itself. You felt that if it had stopped the market would have died, unable to breathe.

Peter threaded his way through the racket, buying what he wanted at half a dozen stalls, haggling for minutes over the odd gura. They came out on the far side of the market, which must once have been sited at the edge of the town, because now beyond it stretched the shanties.

'Can't think why the boss wants you to see the rubbish,' said Peter. 'All just dead-beats and no-goods from now on.'

He strutted along a winding track between tiny shacks, patched together from anything the builders could lay hands on. The morning was hot by now and the air stank. There were no drains. Most huts had reeking latrines, but elsewhere human dung dried in the sun. Lean dogs nosed around. One had evidently died and a dozen kites were squabbling over the body. And everything, the huts, the dung, the dogs and kites, the listless people, was covered with a thin grey film, the salty dust of the Flats on which the shanties were built, endlessly stirred by human movement and endlessly settling again. In the old days, Michael had once told Paul, when a Naga was dying the witch-doctor would paint the sick body all over with ash and have it carried to the compound round the spirit-house so that the blind spirit could find its way to its new home. The grey dust was like that ash. The shanties were that compound. All these tens of thousands of people were just waiting to die.

There was no space between the huts. They were crammed tight together. They spilt out into the road-ways, often blocking them down to a narrow footpath.

'Old Chichaka, he used to send the bulldozers through,' said Peter. 'Clear the roads, see? This new government's too soft for that.'

'Why do they have to build so close? There's plenty of room on the Flats.'

'Got to be near the stand-pipes, see? Government can't put water in for all this trash, all over the Flats. Show you.'

He led the way to where a line of people waited their turn to fill their containers – plastic flasks, jerri-cans, net-slung gourds and pots – at a single tap. There was no jostling, no teasing, no anger. Dully they waited in the broiling sun. Even the babies slung

51

at their mothers' hips were filmed with the death-dust. Paul could see in their faces, in their gestures, in the way they stood, that they knew nothing good was going to happen for them from now on, ever. Full of hope they had left their starving villages, made it somehow across the terrible Flats to Dangoum and the promise of a new, rich life, and this was what they'd found. Paul was glad when Peter asked if he'd seen enough.

Just beyond the edge of the shanties Peter said 'Wait here', and darted into a dark doorway. The house had no windows on to the street. Paul settled into the shade of its wall. After a few minutes a couple of men came out of the door and strolled off, glancing at Paul as they passed. Their eyes rested on him for half a second longer than seemed natural, as if they weren't just noticing him, but looking at him on purpose. Paul wasn't bothered. Peter was obviously vain of his job with Michael, and must have told everyone he was showing the great man's son round Dangoum, but if so why hadn't he taken Paul into the house with him to show off still further? The men had worn jeans and blue T-shirts with notes of music stencilled on, and a little later another three went into the house, wearing the same uniform.

'Some kind of rock group?' he asked when Peter at last emerged, but Peter just laughed.

During the war it was the sort of episode he would have reported automatically on returning from a mission, but Michael didn't get home till after midnight, and anyway the war was over.

The next few days passed dully. Paul found the most amusing thing was to go back to the market and wander around, looking and listening. Michael approved of this. 'Best thing about Dangoum,' he said. 'We're encouraging it all we can. For me it's a kind of symbol – it's what I want for Nagala, that life, that energy, that freedom.'

He gave Paul money to spend. Paul bought a few tapes, and a hunting knife, and had his fortune told by a magic-man who smoked squares of glass over a greasy lamp and peered at the sun through the swirled shapes for messages. Paul was going to be rich and lucky and have five wives and a big Ford car. On the third morning he heard rising above the standard racket an even greater uproar and made his way towards it. The noise came from the barbers' pitch, a space with a few orange crates for customers to sit on, some cracked mirrors, and boards pasted with faded photographs of hairstyles. Two of the barbers had quarrelled and were now circling each other in a half-crouch, cut-throat razors in their hands, spitting insults and challenges while their customers waited half-shaved and the watchers roared them on. A couple of market police with their long truncheons lounged up and stopped to see. The fight never reached bloodshed because one of the deserted customers, a large, calm-looking man in a European suit, tired of the fun, rose from his crate and seized his barber from behind by his left ear and his razor-wrist. The other barber, spotting his chance, rushed in to slash at his enemy but the customer booted him contemptuously in the stomach and he doubled up and dropped to the ground while the customer dragged his own barber away to finish his shave. The audience laughed and cheered.

The laugh at Paul's elbow was so like Jilli's that he

swung round, expecting to find her there, but instead it was a different Fulu girl, two or three years older and in European clothes, but with her hair done into a Fulu top-knot and with tapering hands like Jilli's.

'Hello there,' he said in Fulu.

Her eyes widened, and she answered in the same language.

'Sorry,' he said, 'that's all the Fulu I know. Where did you get these clothes?'

She looked down at her orange satin blouse, tight jeans and high-heeled silver shoes, showing them off to him.

'What's that to you?' she said.

'Only I've got to go back to Tsheba next week, and there's a friend there I'd like to take a present for. She's not quite as big as you.'

'What's her name?'

Jilli's full name was her own and then her mother's and then her grandmother's and so on. He told the girl as much as he could remember. She laughed.

'Sounds funny from a Naga,' she said. 'OK, let's go and look. You got some money?'

They chose a purple blouse for Jilli, good jeans and purple shoes to go with the blouse, and a wide gold belt. Paul bought a silver belt for the girl for helping him. It was nice to have something to spend Michael's money on.

Michael bellowed with laughter when Paul showed him the clothes, and Paul laughed too and tried to explain but that only made Michael laugh still more.

On the fifth day, early in the morning, they drove to the airport and boarded a light plane, taking their bush clothes and a haversack of stores and Michael's big new camera. The sun had not yet risen as they taxied for take-off, but they roared up into its light with Dangoum still in shadow below. The pilot took the plane on a wide circle round the town, gaining height as he did so. Paul gazed down at the sprinkle of lights, still just visible in the dawn shadow, until the sun's rays shot across the plain and drowned them. From up here you could see the whole pattern of the city, as the British had planned it, with Boyo's palace glittering in the middle, surrounded by the ring of high-rises, and the avenues radiating out like spokes through the chequer-pattern roofs of the old town.

When the plane headed west Paul craned to watch the landscape wheeling below. They were following the line of the railway, so it was easy for him to get his bearings and fit it all into the map of Nagala which he carried in his head. They finished with the Flats and roared along above the endless bush. After a while Paul tapped Michael on the shoulder.

'Look,' he said. 'That's where the war ended. That's where I buried my AK.'

'Could be. It's big country, though – easy to get things wrong.'

'No, look, over there, the passing-place for the trains. That's where we were heading to attack.'

'Yes. You're right. If we could have looked into the future that day we'd have seen ourselves flying over right now.'

Later still the note of the engine changed as the plane drifted lower. It circled, rose, came down further on and circled again. The pilot saw what he'd been looking for, made a thumbs-up sign and put the nose down. They landed bumpily on a strip of cleared ground and climbed out into the familiar dusty heat of a bush morning. Paul took huge lungfuls of the clean, dry air. His nostrils crackled with the pleasure of it. He was home.

Three men came running across from where they'd been waiting in the shadow of a grove of umbrella-thorns. They carried hunting spears and wore nothing but tattered khaki breeches. The one in the middle was Papp. He threw his arms round Michael and hugged him and laughed aloud while Michael laughed too and slapped his back. Michael and Paul shook hands with the other two men, who were Papp's half-brothers but spoke no Naga or English. The pilot joined them and they opened some of their stores and ate. Papp's brothers were suspicious of the city food, but kept the cans to use. Together they turned the plane round and watched it take off, then trekked away to meet the rest of Papp's clan.

Three wonderful days followed, just like the war but without the tiredness and tension. They woke in the crisp dawns and breakfasted, and then one of the bush-people would guide them off to find a good place by a water-hole or feeding-ground where they could lie up through the heat of the day and watch the comings and goings of birds and animals and insects, and take photographs. On the second after-noon they joined a hunt, tracking a group of wild pig and surrounding the stand of bitter-grass where they were resting, setting fire to the dried stems and spearing the piglets as they broke cover, everyone screaming with the joy of the hunt-lust. A feast that night round a huge fire, and singing, and the buttock-swinging dances of the bushmen.

On the morning of the fourth day Papp took

Michael and Paul alone to a different part of the bush and showed them a large tree, almost dead except for a few dark spear-shaped leaves at its twig-ends. Everywhere else the gaunt silver-grey branches were festooned with the nests of weaver-birds. Papp made the other two wait fifty yards off while he crawled to the tree and knocked his head against the trunk and chanted and drew signs with his bush-knife in the earth between the spreading buttresses that led down to the roots. Some of the lumps among the branches didn't look like nests, more like bits of carcass a leopard might have dragged up there, but not that either.

'It's his ancestor-tree,' said Michael. 'The clan puts things up there for the ancestors to look after.'

'But Papp's a Christian.'

'He says if Our Lord had lived in the bush he'd have needed an ancestor-tree. Look, isn't that an AK?'

He pointed. Squinting into the strong light Paul saw the familiar barrel and foresight protruding from a fork.

'He's made his war history,' said Michael. 'That's what we've all got to do.'

'How do you tell people?'

'Any way you can. You have an amnesty, and you pay them to bring their guns in. Then you make it a crime to own one, and catch a few people and give them stiff sentences so everyone gets the message. Then you have another amnesty and try again. It's not been going too badly. I don't think there's a lot of guns left in Dangoum.'

When Papp came back to them he said nothing, but led them off to the airstrip, where they ate and talked while they waited for the plane.

'Tell Francis my prayers are for him,' said Papp. 'Tell him to work hard.'

'I don't have to tell him,' said Paul.

'I'll arrange to get him flown down to you next holiday,' said Michael. 'I'm sorry I didn't think of it this time.'

'If he wants to come. But maybe it would be better if he forgot me. He can't belong in this kind of life. He's going to be a great man.'

'Even great men need something behind them,' said Michael. 'Something they can reach out and touch with their minds and know it is real, basic, uncorruptible. Don't you think?'

'You think Malani has that?'

'Malani isn't a great man. He was a good military leader, but peace is too complicated for him.'

'I think the NDR is having too much say. You'll have to do something, or we'll lose what we fought for.'

'Arrangements are being made. We've got to get this OAU heads meeting out of the way. Then you'll see.'

Papp nodded.

'Year ago you were eating porridge with me in the bush,' he said. 'Now you'll be banqueting with the heads of the Organization of African Unity. Sounds just as dangerous.'

'Everything is a risk – doing nothing as much as taking action. There's the plane.'

Papp rose and moved out into the sunlight, shading his eyes and peering at the eastern sky.

'You didn't hear any of that,' said Michael.

'All right,' said Paul.

'Before you go I'll give you a packet, just money

and an address. Maybe a password. I won't say anything about it then, because I'm not sure I can trust Peter. I don't want to fire him now – if he's innocent it wouldn't be fair and if he's spying on me it will alert his bosses. What do you think of him?'

'I don't know. But that day he took me to the market – on the way back from the shanties he told me to wait while he went into a house. I would have told you, only I thought it was something to do with some kind of music group.'

'Why?'

'The men who came out of the house were wearing shirts with music notes on them.'

'Blue T-shirts?'

'Yes. What does it mean?'

'Deathsingers. Chichaka set up a sort of private army of hooligans to beat up anyone in Dangoum who was giving him trouble, so it didn't look as if the police or army were doing it, though everyone knew they were working close with the DDA. Secret police. You've got to have secret police. We've kept the DDA going. Weeded them out, of course, but it's still a problem keeping them in control. They should have known that Deathsingers were going about openly in the Old Town. Perhaps they did know.'

'Is it bad, Michael?'

'Just a bad sign. But at least I now know where I am with Peter. What you've got to do is listen to your radio. If things go badly wrong people may come and pick you up, then try and use you to put pressure on me. So be ready. Make plans. Get Francis back here to Papp if you can.'

'When's it going to happen?'

'The OAU heads are meeting in Dangoum in two

months' time. All the arrangements are made and they won't cancel unless they have to. It's very important to us that they come. It puts Nagala on the world map. All sorts of things. But if the government looks unstable they won't legitimize it by holding their meeting here. As soon as they're gone we'll move.'

Paul nodded. In a way he was glad. Though Michael was obviously on edge and in danger, this was the Michael he knew and worshipped, the planner and leader, the man like the hunting leopard, his whole body still but full of its strength and purpose, while his hand drew in the dust before him. And all the time the buzz of the plane drew nearer.

# Four

Jilli was enchanted by her present. She sat cross-legged on the platform at the back of the house with the clothes laid out on her lap, stroking and stroking them. Then with a sly look she stole off round the ledge and came back a little later wrapped in her red blanket, followed by her grandmother. She peered left and right and out across the reed-beds to make sure no one was watching, then unswathed herself.

Kashka stared, as though he'd never seen her properly before.

'You looking like film star,' he said.

Jilli laughed and wiggled her hips and strutted round the platform, then settled into her grandmother's lap and let the old woman stroke and feel the strange clothes while they chortled together.

'You coming to Hilton, Paul,' she said. 'I giving for you all best best foods, no pay.'

It was strange to Paul to give someone such easy pleasure. His life had had no room for that sort of experience before. He could feel Kashka's jealousy too – Kashka had been away for the holiday, but hadn't thought to bring a present back, or had the wish to have done so till this moment. After a bit Paul told Jilli to go and take the clothes off and hide them. There was no point in making a friend of her if at the same time he made an enemy of her father.

*

School settled into its routine. The marshes shrank so that the reed-beds seemed to grow taller and the channels between them showed more clearly. The main mosquito season was over, but everyone took chloroquin still and smeared themselves with repellent before going down from the dry hillsides to the Strip. Paul listened twice a day to the World Service news, but there was nothing about Nagala except for mentions of the OAU meeting in a few weeks' time. Michael wrote every week but sent no hint of what might be happening. Some of the envelopes looked as if they'd been opened and re-sealed.

'Be ready,' he'd said. 'Make plans.' Where could you hide round Tsheba? In front were the marshes. In the desert to the north you'd die. East or west along the Strip you'd stand out like a zebra among buck. Michael's package was no obvious help – two hundred dollars, three thousand Nagala gurai, an address, 300 Curzon Street, and a password. Paul told Sister Felicity he was thinking of becoming a doctor and asked if he could help in the medicine tent. He gave her time to learn to trust him, then stole chloroquin, repellent and sterilizing tablets. At other times he collected stores – matches, cord, a cooking pan, a plastic water flask and so on. Nothing he couldn't easily carry. Three weeks passed.

It was the first item on the 6 a.m. news on the Thursday of the fourth week. 'Reports are coming through from Dangoum of the attempted assassination of Colonel Malani, Prime Minister of Nagala . . .'

Paul had the volume down and listened under his blanket to the whisper. The rest of the school was woken at half-past six but he'd trained himself to wake early. The other headlines and then back to

Nagala. They didn't know much. A mine on the road back from Olo, and an ambush. Cabinet Ministers in the party. State of Emergency declared. Conflicting reports whether Malani was alive or dead. Then Our Africa correspondent talking about disagreements in the regime following the cease-fire. Malani's failure to control NDR corruption. Public disappointment after early promise . . . Nothing about Michael. While the rest of his tent was still sleeping Paul packed his satchel, then got up and dressed with the other boys. Thursday was a morning for going down to Jilli's, if they were still going. He managed to queue three times for lunch-packs. The headmaster, Mr Salinka, came into Assembly arguing furiously with his deputy, Dr Gonzales. All the teachers must know by now, surely, and some of the other boys had radios, though they mostly used them to listen to music. Mr Salinka conducted Assembly as if nothing unusual had happened, but the teachers behind him whispered all the time among themselves.

The buses came late, and the ride to the Strip was a clamour of rumour and argument. Paul sat silent, but when the bus dropped them and they were standing in the steamy heat beside the ditch Kashka looked east along the track, squared his shoulders and said 'OK, now I'm getting out.'

'Where are you going?' said Paul.

'Baroba.'

'You got any money?'

'A bit of gurai.'

'You'll never make it to Baroba.'

Kashka snorted defiantly.

'Fifty miles to the end of the Strip,' said Paul. 'Think any Fulu are going to help a Baroba? After

that bad, dry bush. Road-blocks on all the bridges –
you'll need more than a few gurai for them. And anyway you don't know what's happening in Dangoum.
Maybe everything's OK. Maybe all this is just getting
shot of the old NDR gang. Francis and me, we're
going to Jilli's to listen for some more news. I've
brought my radio.'

Kashka stared at him, still too proud for advice.

'My father gave me money, case something like
this happened. If we've got to run, we'd best go
together.'

'We'll go to Jilli's,' said Kashka, as if he was giving
the orders.

Paul smiled at Francis, who'd said nothing all this
while. His schoolbook cleverness was no use to him
now.

'We'll look after you,' said Paul. 'It'll all work out
in the end.'

Francis nodded and put his hand into Paul's like a
baby. They walked across the fields and gangways to
Jilli's house, where they settled as usual on the platform and turned the radio on. It was a programme
called *Anything Goes* on the World Service, one of
Jilli's favourites, so she pouted when Paul tuned
across to Radio Dangoum. Military music there, just
like during the war when the government had used
the station for propaganda, with brass bands in
between. Colonel Malani's regime used it for propaganda too, but preferred Afro-Cuban.

'Try Voice of America,' said Kashka. 'It'll be mostly lies, but they might tell us something.'

'What's the wavelength?'

Kashka shrugged. Paul looked at his watch. Ten
minutes before the next World Service bulletin. He

was reaching for the tuning-knob when the music stopped and a woman's voice spoke in English.

'This is Radio Dangoum. We present the Right Honourable Major Basso-Iskani, head of the provisional government of Nagala.'

Paul raised his eyebrows to Kashka, who shook his head. He didn't recognize the name either. A man's voice now spoke, also in English, but heavy and slurred, on a single note, and stumbling as though he was reading the words and wasn't used to doing that.

'Citizens of Nagala. It is with great reluctance that I take the reins of government into my hands. I say I do not do this willingly. I am a plain soldier, not interested in politics. But I am also a patriot, and when I see my beloved country, Nagala, in danger, it is my duty to act.

'The danger is not from outside enemies, but from those within. Some of these enemies are corrupt men, who steal and take bribes, and fill their pockets with money that belongs to our poor country. These I will seek out and punish severely.

'Other enemies are the tools and jackals of foreign powers, who work for the ruin of Nagala, so that when all order and discipline is lost they will have the excuse to send their armies in and take over.

'But from today there will be no more corruption, no more misrule. A Council of State, with myself as its head, will take over. Its proclamations will have the force of law. Those hindering the Council or its agents in the course of their duties will be committing a criminal act, for which the penalty is death.

'A state of emergency is declared, and the so-called free democratic elections scheduled for December are cancelled. When truly democratic elections become possible they will take place, and I and my Council will joyfully surrender power.

'Those responsible for the misdeeds of the deposed government of Colonel Malani will be put on trial, so that their criminal activities may be known to the world.

'To our friends outside Nagala I say this. My government represents the true interests of all the people of Nagala, and the true interests of Africa. In particular I look forward to receiving the delegates to the Organization of African Unity in Dangoum next month, so that I may greet them like a brother and explain to them the reasons for my actions.

'I, Major Dan Basso-Iskani, have spoken. Long live Nagala and the Supreme Military Council!'

The band played *Nagala the Beautiful, Land of the Free*. Another voice started to repeat the message in Naga. Paul turned the volume down and sat motionless, as the chill of shock washed through him. Malani was dead. Michael was dead or in prison. Everything was over.

'What coming?' whispered Jilli. 'This be bad-bad thing, Paul?'

Paul shook his head. His breath came and went in slow sighs. He was trying to force himself to think rationally when Kashka said, 'Paul, you knew this was on. Kagomi gave you money.'

'Not for this. You think he'd help kill Malani? All he told me was he was trying to get rid of the old NDR gang.'

'Looks like they've done the getting rid. We'd better clear out.'

Paul nodded and turned to Jilli.

'Jilli, you're my friend,' he began, but at that

moment she held up her hand and cocked her head to listen. The wash of voices from the fields had hushed and a single voice, far off, was calling in a wailing yodel. Jilli rose and sidled round the hut. The call ended and another voice began, nearer. Paul looked at his watch again and saw that it was after the hour. Hurriedly he re-tuned and turned the volume up. The newsreader was just finishing the headlines.

'. . . scandal is threatening the Japanese government. There has been an explosion in Londonderry, but no casualties.

'The situation following the military coup in Nagala is still confused, but it now seems certain that Colonel Malani, President of the interim government and leader of the Nagala Liberation Army, died in an ambush yesterday as he was returning from Olo to the capital, Dangoum. A mine is said to have exploded under his car, followed by an exchange of fire between his escort and marksmen lying in wait by the road. It is not clear how many were killed, but Dr Alinoko, Minister of Development, and Mr da Paroi, Minister of Finance, are thought to be among them. Now here is our Central Africa correspondent, David Symes, speaking from Kampala.'

A new voice.

'The military coup against the regime of the late Colonel Malani, though sudden, was not wholly unexpected. Certain imbalances and discontents had become increasingly apparent. The presence in the regime of members of the old NDR party was deeply resented by junior leaders of the NLA, and there have been rumours of an attempt to oust them, perhaps with the tacit support of Colonel Malani himself. It is not yet clear whether the NDR has decided to move

67

first, or whether Major Basso-Iskani is acting on his own initiative.

'Little is known of the new leader, but from his name he appears to be a Gogu, a member of a small but warlike tribe from the eastern highlands who were extensively recruited into the army under British colonial rule. The Gogu have a long history of enmity with the much more numerous Baroba, who formed an important section of the NLA. The deposed dictator of Nagala, General Boyo, was himself a Gogu. In his broadcast to the nation Major Basso-Iskani . . .'

Then a summary of the broadcast, and then . . .

'The reference to the forthcoming meeting of the OAU in Dangoum is of interest. It must be doubtful whether this will now take place. The OAU will not wish to appear to legitimize a government that has taken power by force, but on the other hand Dangoum was only accepted as a venue for the meeting after complex negotiations among the competing factions within the OAU and it will be difficult to find an alternative. Provided that Major Basso-Iskani's government can make some show of respectability over the next few weeks the OAU may decide, however reluctantly, to accept the *fait accompli*.'

'That was David Symes, speaking from Kampala,' said the newsreader. 'The latest American trade figures . . .'

Paul switched off. He felt numb, stupid. Francis was crying.

'He is Gogu, then,' said Kashka, and spat.

Jilli came softly back.

'Men going up to school,' she said. 'Soldier men. You hear these callings?'

68

She held up her hand for silence. The yodelling cry was dwindling away west.

'They'll be after you, Paul,' said Kashka. 'Kagomi's son.'

'Jilli,' said Paul. 'Are you my friend?'

She smiled but held her head sideways and watched him out of the corners of her eyes, a yes-and-no look. He began to explain, keeping the words short, the sentences simple.

'My father, Michael Kagomi, is a big man in Dangoum. Colonel Malani is his friend. Now bad men have killed Malani. What have they done to my father? I don't know. These soldiers have come to Tsheba. They are looking for me. Maybe they will kill me. Maybe they will say to my father "Look, we've got your son. Now you do what we tell you". What can I do? Where can I go? That way's no good. That way's no good.'

He pointed east and west along the Strip and north towards the desert.

'I must hide in the marshes,' he said. 'Jilli, you're my friend. You say to your father "Sell a boat to Paul". Look, I've got dollars. Plenty. Please, Jilli. You're my friend.'

Jilli had stopped smiling and was looking at him more sidelong than ever.

'Where you going?' she said. 'Dangoum?'

'Maybe,' said Paul. He hadn't thought about much beyond hiding in the marshes, but the address Michael had given him was in Dangoum. He'd have to go there in the end.

'OK,' said Jilli. 'I come too.'

She slipped away round the hut. There was silence in the fields now, a sense of listening. Far off, like birdsong, another yodelling cry arose. How much time had he got? They'd round up the children still at Tsheba, pick out the ones whose fathers were NLA, then if they'd got a list find that Paul Kagomi was missing . . .

Jilli appeared, leading her grandmother and carrying a decorated pot.

'Take off these clothes,' she said. 'Make you Fulu boys. Quick, quick.'

She shoved the pot under Paul's nose. It contained a slop of grey paste. Reluctantly he stripped and let Jilli push him into a sitting position, cross-legged in front of the grandmother, who gripped his hair and with her other hand started to spread the paste unhurriedly over his face, chanting as she did so, a low, throbbing repetitive sound. The paste was cool on his skin and the movement of the firm old fingers eased some of the tension away. When the grandmother signalled him to stand he opened his eyes and saw that Jilli had gone, but that there were several of the boat-shaped headbaskets which the Fulu used to carry their goods stacked by the ladder. She reappeared carrying a jerrican which she dumped by the baskets, then scampered off again, returning with a rope of mealie-cobs. She made trip after trip to load the baskets.

By the time the grandmother had finished smearing Paul's legs the clay was drying on his face and shoulders, making the skin tingle gently. As she started on Francis, Paul moved away and picked up the jerrican. It was full.

'Are you taking the boat with the motor?' he said. 'What'll your father say?'

Jilli shrugged. She had finished with her father. He was a fool.

'He go find boat,' she said. 'Now you give me dollars.'

'How much?'

She twittered Fulu and the grandmother answered. Jilli couldn't count in Naga yet, so she held up her spread fingers ten times.

'Far too much,' said Paul angrily. 'If we're taking the boat with the motor I'm not buying it. I just want it a few days.'

They bargained to and fro. The grandmother pasted Francis and started on Kashka. In the end they settled for forty dollars, which Paul counted out in fives. Jilli peeled off one note and rolled it into a tight tube which she threaded into her top-knot. The rest she passed to her grandmother.

All this while fresh snatches of news had been floating across the fields. Now a longer message was on the way. Jilli slipped off round the hut to listen. Paul climbed down into the nearest boat and told Francis to pass him down the stores. They were still at it when Jilli's head poked over the edge of the platform.

'Soldier men coming,' she gasped. 'In Tsheba they kill. Bang-bang-bang.'

The shots exploded from her lips, rapid-fire. She passed the last of the stores down, then followed Francis down the ladder, and carried the jerrican over the rocking raft of boats to the one with the motor in it. Paul and Francis worked their way across more slowly, passing the stores from one boat to the next and then moving on. Jilli went back and chose four paddles.

The fields were silent as they sat on the edge of the platform and waited for the grandmother to finish pasting Kashka. Shooting at Tsheba, thought Paul.

Who was there to shoot? Nuns, schoolteachers, children? The BBC man had said that this Basso-Iskani wanted to show the OAU heads he wasn't a thug. Maybe, but Tsheba was a long way from Dangoum, and these were government soldiers. Shooting and burning was all they understood. Or perhaps they'd just fired a few bursts into the air, to show they meant business.

Into the hot and steamy silence came a noise, unmistakable, the roar of a large engine as the driver changed gear to take the hairpin on the last steep slope off the hills. Jilli ran across the platform and snatched the pot of clay from her grandmother's lap.

'Finishing in boat,' she said. 'Quick, quick!'

She twittered a snatch of Fulu, kissed the old lady on the forehead and ran to the ladder. The boys followed. Kashka's left leg was still black from the knee down. Jilli cast off and Paul and Kashka nudged the boat out with their paddle-butts and then spun it round.

There was no time to rig the motor. They knelt by the thwarts and all four paddling together drove towards the nearest channel into the reeds. The bulky boat had its own natural speed and once it had reached that no amount of effort would push it much faster. They seemed to be loitering across the oily, motionless water while the sound of engines – clearly more than one of them now – came nearer and nearer. Three shots rang out before they were halfway to the reeds, and Jilli missed her stroke and craned round.

'OK, OK,' called Kashka. 'Not shooting at us.'

Half a mile away still, thought Paul. Jilli was still staring back, her mouth open, her look appalled. This was new in her world. Then she gripped her paddle, straightened their course and didn't look round again till they reached the reeds.

As soon as they were out of sight they rested, panting. By now the cries from the shore had become screams. There were more shots, several bursts, and then another familiar sound from the old days, the sudden booming roar of a hut going up in flames. Above the reed-beds a billow of yellow smoke exploded into the steam-grey sky. Jilli leaped to her feet and craned to see.

'Ai! Ai!' she gasped. 'They burn houses. Ai! No!'

Kashka shrugged. Like Paul he had seen too many burnt villages to think this astonishing.

'Shall I have a go at the motor?' he said.

'Do you know how?'

'We did a course one base-camp.'

He edged past Jilli, and lifted one end of the ancient object. Paul took the other and together they hefted it aft. The boat rocked wildly with their efforts. The reeds at the stern were woven to a neat but fragile-looking point.

'Don't see how it fits on,' said Paul.

'Must go somewhere,' said Kashka.

Paul turned. Jilli would know. She must have watched her father rigging the motor a hundred times. She was sitting in the bottom of the boat now, shuddering and shaking, with the clay on her face channelled with falling tears. He sighed. That there should be whole stretches of Nagala where the war had never come! That there should be people, thousands and thousands of them, who had never known what it was like! He teetered towards her, knelt and put his arm gently round her shoulders. She looked up and stared at Kashka.

'What's he doing?' she said.

'Fitting the motor,' said Paul. 'Can't see how it goes.'

She straightened her spine. He could sense her effort of will as she heaved herself out of her grief and shock. She felt beneath the pile of stores and eased out a long narrow bundle of stout reeds, lashed together to make a rigid pole. A grass rope was tied to one end. She slotted the pole across the boat so that the part with the rope projected about a metre, then took the further end of the rope aft and looped it over a stubby sort of reed hook. A shorter reed bundle fitted below the pole against the side of the boat.

'Motor goes here,' she said, patting the main pole.

The boys carried it forward again and lashed it in place as she told them. Kashka filled the tank from the jerrican, but when he put out his hand to open the petrol valve she stopped him.

'Not like this,' she said. 'You making it sick, this way.'

With delicate fingers she adjusted the controls and part-flooded the carburettor. Then she spread her hands and said what was obviously some kind of charm or blessing. She handed Kashka the starter cord.

'Now you pull,' she said. 'Three times. Then it goes.'

She was right. At the third pull the motor caught, sputtered while she juggled with the throttle and choke, and at last steadied, drowning all sounds. She rose and looked towards the shore. Now above the reed-beds they could see five separate smoke-pillars rising, and as they watched another hut went up.

They couldn't hear the explosion above the racket from the motor, but the faint thud of air reached them as the smoke-cloud shot skyward. Jilli stared for another few seconds, then set her jaw and crouched down by the motor, pushing Kashka firmly aside. She opened the throttle and the boat surged forward.

Paul studied the reeds looking for a side-turning that might take them clear of the buffalo-pound, but when he pointed towards a promising one Jilli shook her head and steered firmly up the main channel. In a few minutes they reached the pound. This was an area round a low mud island, ringed with an under-water stockade made of reed-stems as thick as your arm to keep the crocodiles out. When Paul had been before, there had been teams of smaller children working continuously along the stockade checking that the fence was sound, and shouting as they did so and splashing the water with their paddles to frighten the crocodiles away, while the older children had been raking waterweed from the surrounding channels, loading it into the boats and ferrying it back to dump it over the stockade for the buffalo to browse. Today, all of them, thirty or so, were gathered on top of the mound, craning aghast towards the shore.

For the moment they didn't seem to have noticed the boat, and left to himself Paul would have tried edging round the clearing and reaching the far side of the stockade unaided, but Jilli headed straight for the entrance gap. Paul crawled aft.

'Why are we going in here?' he shouted.

'My brother, my brother!' said Jilli.

She had three brothers, but Paul knew she was talking about the oldest one, Muliku. One day he would be head of the family, and already he had a lot of authority among the other children. From the first he had been deeply suspicious and resentful of the three strangers, and he would never approve of Jilli running away with them, or borrowing the boat with the precious engine.

'He can't do anything against guns,' said Paul. 'They'll shoot him as soon as they see him.'

'My brother, he knows the ways in the marsh,' said Jilli, miming with a sinuous arm towards the south.

Paul gave in. His plan of escape had not in fact got further than buying or stealing a boat and hiding in the marshes, and when the immediate danger was over working his way along by the Strip and round past the road-blocks at the bridges, and then coming ashore and hitching a lift down the highway. South of the marshes was Fulu territory, but a different sort of Fulu living in fishing villages, and beyond that the enormous central expanse of bush, with the railway running across it. Now his instincts, all his knowledge, drew him towards the bush. And somewhere down there, twelve miles south of the railway, his AK was buried.

The moment the bow touched land Jilli was scampering up the mound. She had a bundle under her arm. The herders came rushing to meet her, yelling questions, then ringed her while she answered, throwing her arms out in wide emphatic gestures. They turned all at once and stared at the boys in the boat. Muliku came striding down towards the shore, but Kashka had kept the motor running and immediately backed out. When Muliku waded into the water Paul drew out his hunting knife and stood up, ready, but Jilli paddled out beside her brother, took him by the elbow and tugged him back to dry land.

A fierce argument began between them, watched by the boys from the boat and the herders from the mound above. Muliku was older and stronger than Jilli, but she didn't seem at all afraid of him, rising on tiptoe to gesture and yell until he backed away and made calming signals with his hands.

Jilli paid no attention, in fact she seemed to have worked herself into a state of pure frenzy, but then all of a sudden she paused and stood motionless for several seconds. Slowly, moving like a priest or a dancer, she unfastened her blue bead belt and dropped it at Muliku's feet. She unrolled her bundle. Inside the thin grass mat were the clothes Paul had given her. She pulled the blouse over her head, stepped delicately into the jeans, closed the zip and fastened the waist-clip. She buckled the wide gold belt in place and slipped the shoes on, then stood with her hands on her hips, silent, staring at her brother.

He stared back, began a gesture of appeal and broke it short. The children above watched in silence, as though what Jilli had done was somehow equal to the horrors on the shore. At last Muliku bowed his head and turned away to a pile of fresh-cut reeds. He chose several long, thin stems which he began to plait together in an irregular pattern while Jilli stood at his elbow watching intently. Sometimes he spoke. Sometimes she asked a question and he would answer briefly. The herders returned to the top of the mound to watch the shore. Yells and shouts and sounds of burning, with occasional shots, came steadily through the heat-haze. Paul waited, wary, watching in case any of the herders took a boat from the far side of the mound and tried to work round and cut them off. None did.

After about twenty minutes Muliku knotted the last reed-ends tight and handed her what he had made, an odd-shaped woven mat a few inches wide and a bit over two feet long. She studied it and asked a question, pointing at a particular section. He explained. She put out her hand and stroked his arm, gently, while she said what was obviously some kind of goodbye, but he stood unheeding, motionless as a sleeping kite.

His head turned to watch Jilli but he did nothing to stop her as Kashka brought the boat in and she stepped aboard, settling into the bows in a kneeling position so that she could point the best way between the groups of wallowing buffalo. They reached the entrance gap and turned along the outside of the stockade. Looking towards the mound Paul saw that the other herders were leaving the mound now and getting into their boats, but Muliku was still where they had left him, standing at the water's edge with his head bowed and weighing the blue bead belt in his hand.

The mat Muliku had woven was something between a map and a code, so that Jilli, by following a particular stem through the pattern, could tell which turnings to take. The *put-put* of the motor drowned all other sounds. Morning moved to noon, becoming steadily hotter and steamier. The air swarmed with insects, buzzing and hovering and trying to bite through the coat of clay which covered their skins. Jilli undressed and used the last of the paste to renew the coat on her legs where she had waded into the water and to finish off Kashka. They stopped the motor so that they could listen to the midday bulletin, but there was nothing new.

Paul got out his map and did sums. It was about sixty miles across the marshes in a straight line, but judging by the sun Jilli seemed to be taking a bit of an angle, and there were twists and turnings of the channels to allow for. Say ninety. Between two and three days if the petrol lasted. Four if they had to paddle far. There was water all around and plenty of sterilizing tablets, which was just as well, as the clay, once it had dried, was porous, so it worked a bit like a cooling jar, almost sucking the sweat out of you and evaporating it, helping to keep your body-heat down but making you endlessly thirsty. For food there were Jilli's stores, and five packed lunches from the school. Jilli's mealie-cobs would need cooking, so were no use till they reached shore, but there was a sort of mealie-cake the Fulu made – you had to moisten it down before you could eat it, and then it was like the porridge the commando used to live off in the bush.

In mid-afternoon the engine stopped. Overheated, Kashka thought. He and Jilli and Paul paddled while they waited for it to cool, but Francis was very listless and slept. When Kashka got the motor started again Jilli wove a fish-trap and trailed it over the side but didn't catch anything. Not all the way was channels and reed-beds. There were large open stretches through which a sluggish current sometimes moved. Towards dusk they passed islands with mangroves growing into the water, and at one point a tongue of naked rock on which thirty or forty crocodiles lay basking in the last of the sun. The reed-beds were full of small birds, and fish-hawks wheeled serenely over the open stretches.

As the sun went down Jilli chose a stand of reeds and told Kashka to steer straight at it and stop the motor when they reached it. As the bow nudged in they grabbed the stems and hauled the boat forward until it was completely hidden. They ate the spare school lunches and some mealie-cake for supper and Paul dished out an extra ration of chloroquin, waking Francis up and forcing him to swallow his. There was still nothing new on the World Service, and Radio Dangoum was just brass bands and boastings. They all slept badly. In the middle of the night the boat rocked as a herd of hippos passed along the channel they'd been using.

The morning news named the dead ministers, but said nothing about Michael. There was an interview with the secretary of the OAU, who refused to say whether the Dangoum conference was going to be cancelled. Jilli had caught a nice fat fish in her trap, which she put back in the water, fish and all, so that it would still be fresh when they got a chance to cook it. By now Francis was clearly sick, his lips fat and mottled yellow and purple. He wouldn't eat but Paul forced him to drink and swallow another chloroquin.

They used the motor all day, managing it more carefully this time so that it didn't overheat. At noon they landed on an island, made a fire with the mealie-shucks and roasted strips of fish to eat with the mealie-cake. That night Francis moaned continually, and Paul sat up by him, trying to dribble water between the swollen lips.

'Why bother?' said Kashka. 'He's dying, isn't he?'

'No!' muttered Paul. 'He's got to live, I'm going to see he does. One day he's going to be Prime Minister of Nagala. My father, Michael Kagomi, said so.'

Kashka snorted surprise, turning the snort into a

sneer, but he said nothing more about letting Francis die.

The next morning news barely mentioned Nagala. The jerrican had to be tilted right over and still didn't fill the tank. Well before noon the engine spluttered and died, while the marsh seemed to stretch on ahead of them, all the same, endless. Jilli wasn't worried. She held up Muliku's mat and put her finger an inch from the top.

'We're here,' she said. 'We're going just to here.'

They paddled on, two at a time, taking turns, while Francis lay in the bows shaded by grass mats which Jilli had strung for him between the thwarts. He had stopped moaning, but as he breathed bubbles of froth came and went in his nostrils. By mid-afternoon when Paul rose to change places he could see through gaps in the nearer reeds a low line of something in the distance ahead which wasn't also reeds. Jilli caught another fish. The water became blacker, so that in places they were forcing the boat through what was almost soft slime. The channel they were in turned, widened, and they were looking at trees, a long dark line of them rising from a network of roots above the water.

Jilli made them paddle another hour along the shore to an inlet where they forced the boat between reed-stems and found dry land. Paul stepped ashore and looked round. There was a faint path running away south, but it showed no signs of recent use. It was only an hour till sunset.

'OK,' he said. 'Let's camp here tonight and go on tomorrow.'

Jilli shook her head and gestured at the trees.

'No, no,' she said. 'My brother said "Don't sleep in this place. You'll all get sick".'

Paul gave in at once. Michael had used local guides when he could, and had trusted their warnings. They unloaded their stores, stowed the motor and covered it with mats, then pushed the boat back into the reeds to hide it. Paul picked Francis up in the hold that the Warriors had been taught for carrying a wounded comrade. Jilli led the way up the path.

The belt of trees turned out to be only a few hundred yards wide, and beyond it, mile after mile, stretched the familiar brown and grey and yellow landscape of the bush. Almost at once they reached a cleared level of dust with tyre marks running across it. The map had shown a road along the southern edge of the marsh. This would be it.

He caught Jilli by the elbow as she started to cross and told her to follow him, stepping in his footsteps, so that they didn't break any of the tyre tracks. Kashka came last, twisting back and using a branch broken from a bush to wipe the footprints away. This was something you did, always. Any tracker could still have told that someone had crossed the road here, but no one in a passing truck would notice, whereas they would certainly have seen footprints or a break in the tyre tracks.

Paul led on into the slowly rising bush till he found a suitable hollow. Wearily he eased Francis down and looked around him. This would do. They'd need a fire, and the sides of the hollow would hide the flames. Anyway he couldn't carry Francis much further.

It was like the old days. They gathered wood and lit a fire and roasted Jilli's fish and ate it with hot mealie. Francis woke and managed to swallow a few tiny mouthfuls. Then they sat in the dark, feeding the fire and watching the flames.

'What are you going to do next?' said Kashka.

'Head south to the railway,' said Paul. 'See if I can jump a train with Francis and get out towards Shidi. There's someone'll look after him there. Then I'll head for Dangoum and find what's happened to my father. What about you?'

'I'll go to Baroba. Look for my friends.'

'Got enough money to buy a ride?'

'I'll walk.'

'It's a hell of a distance, and there's bound to be at least one road-block you can't walk round, at the Oloro bridge. I'll show you my map. I could give you some gurai.'

'You're going to Shidi, Paul?' said Jilli. 'Where's Shidi?'

He explained. She stared at him, hurt and angry.

'In my house you said you're going straight to Dangoum.'

'Never said straight.'

'OK. I'll go with Kashka.'

'I'm not going to Dangoum. Don't want a girl with me, either.'

'Then I'm going alone.'

'No you're not,' said Paul. 'You're not going any-where alone. You know what'll happen to you – first couple of men who find you wandering about, they'll rape you, maybe kill you. Dangoum's the same. I've been there. Full of bad men. Right, Kashka?'

'Damn right,' said Kashka. 'You just wait till your father comes for the boat and go back with him to the Strip.'

'No, no, no! Paul, you said you're my friend! Why are you saying this now?'

Both boys started to argue with her, but by now she

was too upset to manage either Naga or English. She stood up, stammering a mixture of all three languages, gesturing with her whole body as she mimed the scene when she'd stripped off her belt and given it to Muliku, and dressed in her western clothes. Paul saw that that must have meant more than he'd realized at the time. By doing it she'd somehow cut herself off. If she tried to go back to the Strip her family would have nothing to do with her. What about persuading Kashka to take her with him at least as far as the Oloro crossing? She might make it down to Dangoum, and find Fulu people among the shanties to take her in. But suppose on the way she met some gang of near-bandits, raiders or poachers or the sort of thugs who'd claimed to be soldiers during the war as an excuse for pillage and murder – if Malani was dead that would all be starting again now – she wouldn't last a day. He sighed.

'OK,' he said. 'You come along by me. When old Francis better, we going south.'

She laughed with relief and sat down. The night grew colder and they piled more wood on the fire. Jilli had brought one blanket, under which she and Francis and whichever of the boys wasn't on watch huddled and tried to sleep, but Paul would have been wakeful even without the cold and the hard ground. He had no trouble keeping his eyes open during his stints on watch. The mist from the marshes blurred the northern stars so he faced the other way and watched the familiar constellations, huge and calm, wheel steadily westward. He felt fulfilled, confident. He had done what Michael had asked him, made plans, and when the crisis struck, used them, taking his chances as they came. Francis was not going to die. Paul would get him to Papp, who would take over that responsibility, and then he would head for Dangoum. He had no notion what he would do when he got there, or how he could help Michael, but Michael had given him an address, and that was enough. Meanwhile he had come home. Though he had never been within a hundred miles of the hollow where he now sat and watched, he was where he belonged. The old night noises, the far whoop of a jackal, the creak of moonbugs calling for mates, the rustle and skitter of foraging little mammals, all these told him that this was the bush, with himself part of it, living in it, moving through it, skilful, alert, leaving no tracks, a Warrior.

We'll be going down to the railway, he thought. I can leave Jilli there to watch the line and look after Francis while I go and get my gun.

# Five

The first thing Paul saw when he woke was Jilli sitting outlined against the white dawn sky at the rim of the hollow, weaving grass stems together with long, quick-moving fingers. Francis was still asleep, his breath steady, his lips less bruised-looking than yesterday. Paul rolled stealthily clear and doubled the blanket over him.

Kashka had vanished, but in a couple of minutes he appeared dragging a dead branch. There were several others stacked by the fire.

'You're not going then?' whispered Paul.

'After breakfast. But if you're going to give me some cash I'll bring a bit of wood for you.'

Kashka didn't smile – he didn't seem to know how – but it was a sort of half-joke. He was too proud to accept money for nothing, but at the same time he'd have to carry wood for a fortnight to earn as much as he'd need. Paul laughed.

'My thanks,' he said. 'You'd better have a look at the map.'

He got it out and spread it flat.

'We're about here,' he said. 'That's the main Oloro bridge – I don't know if they've mended the south one. There'll be road-blocks in any case. They might be on the look-out for kids who've got away from Tsheba.'

'Not so likely this side of the marshes. If I dash them a few gurai . . .'

'It's a long way. More than three hundred miles.'

'OK,' said Kashka confidently.

He studied the map a while, grunted and began to put his belongings together. Paul counted him out three hundred gurai and added a five dollar bill – he'd need to get to a fair-sized town before he could change that.

'My thanks,' said Kashka.

He rose and stood picking at the layer of clay on his forearm. It came away in tiny flakes, leaving the skin mottled like the scales of a snake.

'I'm going down to the creek to wash this off,' he said.

'Hadn't you better keep it till you're clear of Fulu country?'

'Not if I can't speak Fulu. Anyway Jilli says you've got to take it off after four days or your skin goes bad. Well, I'm off. Good luck. Be lucky, Jilli.'

He picked up his satchel and strode out of sight.

An hour later when he crossed the road Paul saw Kashka squatting in the shade a hundred yards west, waiting. He was wearing T-shirt and jeans, and his uncovered skin was its proper glossy black. Paul wiped out his footprints with extra care as he crossed the road – no truck would stop for a hitch-hiker if there were signs of other strangers around, because even with the war ended you could still meet raiders and brigands. He waved and went on down to the creek.

While he was scraping the softened clay from his chest he heard the sound of an engine, and stood tense. A truck, but not army – you got to know that note. But begging a lift was still a risky business. Kashka would be standing up now, holding out a twenty gura note to show he could pay his fare. The driver would either stop, or speed up if he thought Kashka might be a decoy. He might also calculate whether Kashka was carrying enough money for it to be worth killing and robbing him . . .

The truck slowed, idled just long enough for a passenger to climb aboard, growled on. Another good omen.

Back at the hollow he found that Jilli had put her clothes away and was wearing the thing she'd been weaving, a long grass belt wound four times round her waist, with a neat grass apron in front. He'd seen girls on the Strip wearing belts like that before they were old enough for the blue beads.

'That's pretty,' he said. 'There's a bit of my back I couldn't reach.'

He squatted down while she scraped the last of the clay from between his shoulder-blades, using bits of stiff fern-leaf he'd found by the creek.

'OK,' she said. 'Now I'll go and wash too.'

'What'll you do about new paste?'

'Not going to put it on.'

She pouted at his look of surprise.

'You told Kashka you aren't Naga. You're Nagala, you said. OK, me too. Not Fulu any more. I'm Nagala too.'

They stared at each other. She doesn't know what she's saying, he thought. She doesn't understand anything about the war, and why we're fighting it. All she wants is to get to Dangoum and become a waitress at the Hilton. Then he remembered that five years ago a small boy, wild as a jackal, had crawled into a camp at dawn to steal food. And now he was a Warrior. It was as if Jilli had spoken a password. He smiled and spread his hands in acceptance.

'OK,' he said. 'Now you're a Nagala Warrior, same as me.'

They spent five days in the hollow, waiting for Francis to get well enough to move. He had a relapse on the second day – perhaps he'd caught some kind of chill when they'd washed the clay off him – but on the third morning he woke feeble but clear-headed. Paul would have liked to move camp, because the longer they stayed in one place the more likely it was that some big carnivore would find them, but he couldn't find anywhere as good. So they carried every uneaten scrap at least a hundred yards into the bush and Jilli took turns with Paul to watch at night. She was a Warrior now.

On her very first watch she shook Paul awake and he looked up to see a line of eyes gleaming along the rim of the hollow. He grabbed the spear he'd made by lashing his knife to a strong stick, and counted. Six pairs. Hyena, or wild dog, maybe. Probably too small a pack to overcome their fear of man, and fire. Only you could never tell with wild animals. After a few minutes they ghosted away but he spent the rest of that night on watch.

Next day he trekked several miles along the road and found a Fulu fishing village where there was an old man who could smatter Naga. He bought dried fish, and stale expensive mealie-cake. Jilli had caught fish in her traps at the creek, but they had to be eaten almost at once or they went bad. It was about a hundred miles to the railway, eight days' trek, say. They could carry food for five days, Paul thought, but water for only two or three.

'I would rather come with you to Dangoum,' said Francis. 'That way we could try the road.'

'Michael told me to get you to Papp.'

'If he told you, OK.'

'Anyway the road would be pretty risky. A lot of little dangers all the time, instead of one big one. We're almost all right for food. I don't know about water.'

Paul did know, but he wasn't going to say so. Logically the road must be the better bet. He could find a way of getting Francis out to Shidi from Dangoum. But his fingers yearned for the touch of his AK, a call that was almost too strong for logic.

Squatting on his haunches Francis studied the map by the light of the flames.

'It's bad bush, this bit,' he said. 'Papp told me. But there are three water-holes. His people used to use them when they trekked to the Flats for salt.'

'Where are they?'

'He didn't tell me, using a map. His people didn't like the river people so they went north three days and found water, and then east and found water twice more. Below the hills, he said.'

'Must be where the railway runs.'

'No, not those hills. Another range, further north, I think.'

'Must be these ones here. We should be able to get that far. Then if we can find tracks . . .'

All animals have to drink, most of them every day. Sets of tracks converging on a point should lead to water. Probably.

'What do you think?' said Paul.

'Papp said it was bad bush between the hills. Just bad, not very bad. OK for two or three people, not a whole tribe. He didn't say anything about this side.'

'We can try. Go on a couple of days. If it's no good, come back. Soon as you're strong enough we'll start.'

He explained the position to Jilli, who shrugged.

'If you're going, I'm going too,' she said.

The weight of the short-wave radio was too much to risk on the journey, so they listened to it that evening for the last time. There was one scrap of fresh news about Nagala – the OAU was going to send observers to Dangoum to report back on whether the Heads of State Conference could still take place. It seemed remote, unreal, nothing to do with three children sitting round a fire, ready to set out on a dangerous journey.

They left before dawn, Paul with his satchel over his shoulder, a Fulu basket on his head and his spare hand steadying his spear-pole on his shoulder. Jilli also carried a basket and the other end of the pole, from whose centre hung the jerrican, half-filled with water. They had rinsed and rinsed it, but the water still tasted of petrol. Francis carried his satchel and the plastic flask, half-full. They drank that first.

They did about seven miles before it became too hot to walk, and another five in the afternoon. They could have done more, but towards sundown Francis spotted the wizened stems of a gourd twisting across a patch of bare ground, and they stopped to dig out the fleshy root. The pulp was full of water. It was held together by fibres you had to keep spitting out, and tasted of nothing, but they sucked it until they'd had all the water they'd needed and squeezed the rest into the flask, half-filling it again.

Next morning, as it was getting hot, Francis veered aside to a low rocky mound, which turned out to be riddled with holes. He showed them how to make deadfall traps, large flat stones delicately propped on sticks, with a bit of bait tied to one of the sticks so that when it was tugged the structure collapsed and the stone crashed down. They made several. Jilli was very good at it. They were dozing in the shade of a flame-thorn when they heard the first trap fall. That one caught nothing, but by the time the day started to cool they had killed three plump yellow ground-squirrels.

'What do you think?' said Paul.

'It's bad bush,' said Francis. 'In good bush we'd have seen two or three gourds each day. No termites, either.'

'What are the squirrels living on?'

'Flame-thorn nuts. We can't eat them. And roots which grow into their tunnels.'

'If we hadn't found anything we'd have had to turn back now. If it doesn't get any worse I think we'll be OK.'

So they went on. They found another gourd but no more food. Ahead now they could see a low range of hills, which by the time they camped for the night seemed only a few miles off. They split the ground-squirrels, cleaned them and roasted them whole. The sweet, fatty flesh was delectable.

'Better than you'll find in the Dangoum Hilton, Jilli,' said Paul.

She laughed, the grease round her cheeks glistening in the firelight. It was like the good days in the commando, when the war was quiet. Paul felt full of confidence. The hills were not far off, and there were water-holes on the far side of them. He calculated that he had now reached the point of no return. If they turned back now and found the same amount of food, they should make it to the marshes. If they went on one more morning's march it would be too late. He was going on.

The third day was very bad. In the morning they wasted half an hour and a lot of energy digging down to the root of another gourd, but when the point of Paul's pole struck it, it emitted a foul stink. They looked at Francis.

'Don't know,' he said. 'Papp never showed me.'

Paul touched the gourd and tasted his finger. The juice burnt like fire, though he spat and spat, and the taste stayed in his mouth all day. They trekked on and found nothing. Their eyes had lied, and the hills were further than they'd guessed. They reached them towards sunset and found them ghastly, a bare, pale slope of rock and stone, without bush or blade, stretching east and west as far as they could see. They could find no wood, so slept that night without a fire. Nothing came near them that night, and even that was a bad sign. It meant that nothing lived, or could live, on these hills. It was too late to go back.

In the cool before dawn they started to climb. The sun rose, unveiled by any haze. It bored into the pale rocks, which absorbed its heat and sent it roasting back. By the time they reached the crest, though it was still well before noon, it was hotter than Paul had ever known.

Beyond the ridge lay a stony valley, then another ridge, and the crest of a higher one beyond that. It looked about four miles across the first valley, but knowing now how his eyes lied in this clear air Paul called it eight. Say another eight to the further crest. Sixteen. More than they'd done in a day, so far. Impossible in this heat. The plastic flask was empty, the jerrican dangerously light despite their tiredness. They turned and looked north. No. No hope.

'OK,' said Paul. 'We'll never make it while the sun's up. We'll rest in this bit of shade by that over-hang back there and try it tonight. There's a good moon.'

There was nothing to argue about. They spent the day stretched out in a strip of shadow, which narrowed at noon to less than six inches, but Jilli extended it by dismantling one of the head-baskets and using the rib reeds, their clothes, and the grass mats she'd wrapped her stores in to make a fragile awning. They were naked, but the sweat streamed from them. They drank by sips. There was no breath of wind. At last the long torture eased. The sun red-dened to a huge disc in the copper-coloured west. They decanted the last of the jerrican into the flask and climbed to the crest again, leaving the jerrican and anything else they didn't absolutely have to carry behind.

At the crest they halted and gazed south. If there's another ridge beyond that further one, thought Paul, we're dead.

The sun set as they were starting down. In a few minutes it seemed too dark to see, but then the stars were there, brilliant millions of them, and as their eyes became used to the night they found they could pick their way on. Soon the light strengthened, the stars became fewer, and then the moon was rising, casting hard black shadows you thought you would stumble over.

The air cooled, but the day's heat still streamed up from the rocks and shale, soon with faint tinglings of moisture in it making it bliss to breathe. Paul felt stronger, a bit light-headed, cheerful in spite of the danger. Jilli began to sing.

There was a black gully at the bottom of the valley, eroded tens of thousands of years ago by some stream when these hills had been green. Perhaps there was water still down there, deep under the earth. It took them some time to find a safe way across.

Climbing the slope to the next ridge was not too bad, easier in fact than picking their way down had been in the deceptive light. Though they rested twice on the way up Paul was surprised to find when they reached the crest that the moon was now high over head, the night more than half gone. Looking back and on he tried to estimate distances. Both valleys seemed about the same. There were silverings of mist in the bottom of this one, a promise of dew when dawn came. He could see no sign of yet another crest beyond this next one.

Of course the second valley was harder, not in itself but because they were now so tired. They picked their way down, not fully aware of this, only finding that the slope stretched on and on. At least there was no gulley in the bottom, but the climb up the slope seemed endless. They rested frequently, but the air now was almost freezing and they needed to move to keep warm. Between rest and rest the stars vanished and the sun rose, welcome for half an hour for its warmth on their chilled bodies, but soon an enemy again. By the time they reached the top it was well up.

Shaking with the effort they gazed south. There were no more hills. Below them, stretching beyond sight, lay the bush.

'Look! There!' said Paul.

The others had seen it before he spoke. Everywhere else the bush was its familiar dry-season colour, but there was one patch of pure dark green, close below the hills but several miles away to their left. No need to have had Papp as your uncle to know there must be water there. It seemed so close that it was difficult not to swig the last of the flask and just scamper to that wetness and greenness, but Paul's Warrior training held. He let the others take a few sips, rinsing their mouths round before swallowing, and drank even less himself. Then they started down the now-burning slope.

By the time they reached the level they were exhausted again. Joy was gone, hope almost gone. Numbly they trudged on. Francis was nearly done for. He fell several times. Paul helped him up and put his arm round to steady him, but still he stumbled. Paul would have carried him if he could, but knew he hadn't the strength. Then Francis fell once more, tried to crawl to his feet, collapsed and lay still.

'OK,' said Paul. ''Bout a mile still. Jilli, you stay with Francis. I'll fetch us some water.'

She nodded and he poured the last of the water into the cooking pan and went on alone, carrying the empty flask. The trees were nearer than he'd realized, but desperate for water though he was he crouched by a bush and studied them for several minutes before going in. Anything could be waiting at a water-hole – poachers, soldiers, a leopard. With his knife ready he inched his way into the grove. Above him a gang of parakeets skimmed squealing to a further tree. A good sign – they'd shown no fret till he'd disturbed them. Still wary he stole through the thick, mud-reeking shade.

There were tracks, but too many to read. Between dusk and dawn hundreds – thousands – of creatures would be gathering here to drink. He followed a path they'd made, stopping every few paces to peer around and above. Above would be where a leopard might lie. Nothing, and no sound but the buzz and click of insects and the mutter of heat-stupefied birds among the leaves.

The ground dipped to a hollow of trampled mud with an oily pool at its centre. A black snake was drinking at the far edge. He crept down, undid the flask-cap, took two tablets from his pack and dropped them in, then gently pushed the flask below the surface till the water flowed in. When the flask was two-thirds full he lifted it out and squatted there, waiting for the tablets to dissolve.

There was something wrong. What? Too much stillness? Something he'd seen but not noticed? A smell? As if merely easing his neck he looked up and turned his head to and fro. Nothing. Nothing but silence and heat. Ah. Just beyond the muddy area above the snake were some broken branches lying in a vague heap – bits of *badi*-bush, fat little leaves on grey stems. What were they doing in here? *Badis* had evolved to stand the tropic sun. Michael had shown him how the leathery leaves stored water without losing it to the air, while the roots went twice as deep as the height of the bush to find moisture. They actually needed the blaze and oppression of the sun to grow at all. You'd never find one under a tree.

Swirling the flask, pretending to be just helping the tablets dissolve, he glanced casually at the pile again. There was something in there, a dark gleam. An eye? Too large. A gun? No, a camera! The branches were a hide! For an instant his heart leapt at the thought that Michael himself was lying there, watching the water-hole, just as they'd done together on their visit to Papp. Nonsense, of course.

He rose, drank a few mouthfuls from the flask and stoppered it, but instead of turning back walked on round the pool as though he'd intended all along to be going that way. Passing the hide he peered down into the branches. From this angle the figure with the camera was obvious. One track-shoe was right out in the open.

'Mister, I seeing you foot,' he whispered.

'Uh?' said a voice. 'Hell. And anyway, what are *you* up to, out in these wilds, wearing a watch and speaking English and sterilizing your drinking water?'

'Make him safe for to drink.'

The hide quivered. With a grunt like a wild sow the man backed himself out and sat up. He was red-faced, bald, yellow-bearded.

'Just what I mean,' he said. 'Perfect little sequence, human at one with nature coming to the pool to drink, just like a lion or kudu, only he brings a plastic flask and pops tablets in it. Where are the rest of you? You can't be on your own?'

'My friends back in bush. Francis too tired, so I come fetch water.'

'How far? How many? Why'd they send a kid on?'

The right questions, thought Paul. His friends could be poachers or bandits. Either might murder a man for his good camera.

'Francis fall down,' he said. 'Too tired. We done cross hills. Jilli stayed with him while I go bring water.'

'Kids too? That the lot of you?'

'Sure.'

The man got up.

'Let's fetch your friends in,' he said. 'Come and meet my girl. We'll take the truck.'

He led the way out on the far side of the grove. The truck was parked close against the trees with an awning spread out from its rear end. In its shade a woman was sitting in a folding chair, reading a book. Paul had expected her to be European, like the man, and indeed she was wearing khaki blouse and shorts, and sunglasses pushed up on to her hair. But the hair was glossy blue-black and her skin as brown as Paul's.

'You've missed dinner,' she said, not looking up.

'Fell asleep,' said the man. 'This is Sophia. I'm Joel Funk.'

'I Paul.'

Now the woman looked up.

'Hi, Paul,' she said. 'Where did you spring from?'

'Says he's come across the hills,' said Joel. 'There's a couple of other kids back there somewhere, one of them too done for to make it. OK if I take the truck?'

The woman looked at Paul for some while.

'What's the other side of the hills?' she said.

'Bad bush. Up beyond that, marshes. Other side marshes, the Strip. Then only desert.'

'Yes, I see. He's on the level, darling.'

'Thought so,' said Joel. 'Come along, Paul.'

At the sound of the approaching engine Jilli had tried to hide Francis, but was thrilled by the ride back to

99

the water-hole. By the time they reached it Sophia had a kettle boiling. She immediately took charge of Francis, feeling his pulse, then wrapping him in a light blanket and cradling him while she spooned sweet, tepid, milky tea between his lips. Meanwhile the other two squatted either side of her, sipping their tea from blue enamel mugs.

'Don't give them any more, Joel,' said Sophia. 'They'll take a bit to absorb that. Do you all speak English?'

'Francis speaking damn good,' said Paul. 'Me, OK. Jilli not been at school, so she speaking only a bit.'

'I speaking damn good,' said Jilli. 'Next on the BBC – World News. This is London.'

She had the voice absolutely right. You would have thought there was a radio hidden beside her. Sophia and Joel laughed aloud.

'Jilli must be Fulu by the look of her,' said Sophia. 'You can't be, Paul, or Francis.'

'No. No tribes. Jilli, me, Francis, we be Nagala.'

Jilli nodded. Paul was pleased to see Sophia's eyes widen. She made no comment, but turned and laid Francis carefully in the shade of the tent, covering him with another blanket.

'I think he'll be all right now,' she said. 'Tell me what happened at Tsheba.'

This time Paul felt his own eyes widen.

'How you knowing?' he said.

'I'm a journalist. My assignment with Joel is to make a television feature about the interrelation of people and wildlife in the aftermath of a long-lasting bush war, but I pick up anything I can. We got into Dangoum the day before the coup. We planned to start our work among the bush people north-west of Shidi, but that's still a restricted area . . .'

'I been there,' said Paul.

'You have? Well, people like us need permits, and our main contact was arrested in the coup. When we started asking for him the new regime took an unhealthy interest in us, and it looked as if we might find ourselves deported and our vehicle confiscated, so we decided to head out in the general direction of Shidi, cross-country, and hope they were too busy to come looking for us. But while we were in Dangoum I began to pick up gossip about something nasty having happened at Tsheba, and now Joel comes into our camp with a kid who knows what's north of the hills and speaks English and talks about being at school, not to mention a Fulu girl who can speak pure BBC, and they must have had a reason for making this pretty desperate journey . . . How did you cross the marshes?'

Paul was starting to explain when Francis stirred and woke. Sophia fed him more sweet tea and Joel brought a pack of European biscuits like the ones Paul had eaten in Michael's flat. Jilli got out her own new clothes and put them on and imitated the way Sophia held her mug. Joel lent her some sunglasses and found her a chair to sit in and she chattered away about her plans. Paul watched them under his eyebrows. To trust, or not to trust? They'd trusted him, deciding he wasn't bait sent by bandits to lure them out into an ambush. Joel got out a camera and filmed Jilli, clearly because she amused him, but Sophia took her more seriously and began to say almost what Michael had said, that she'd do much better if she learnt to write and type. That decided

101

him. He waited for a pause, then held up his hand to interrupt.

'Sorry,' he said. 'This man, going for find you permit, then they putting him in prison – this be Michael Kagomi?'

'That's right,' said Joel. 'He'd set it all up, including a guide the other end . . .'

'Papp?'

'Jeez, Paul! You in the secret police?'

'My father, Michael Kagomi.'

'I didn't know he was married,' said Sophia.

'My mother, the war.'

'Oh, I see. You're one of those? I was thinking of doing a feature on kids like you, and how you're settling in.'

'Francis too. When we finding him, we say Papp now be uncle for him. Michael same for me, only when war done end he saying to me "Now I become father for you, and you same son for me." But you telling me for sure he be in prison?'

'Nothing's for sure after a coup. That's just what we heard. We took a special interest in him, remember.'

'They got him in these cells under old palace, you guess?'

'I wouldn't think so. I did that tourist bit last time I was in Dangoum. There's only about a dozen cells down there, and they've got getting on a hundred top people detained. I should think it's more likely the DDA – that's the secret police, you know – have got him in one of their barracks somewhere.'

'You think they going to kill him?'

Sophia shrugged.

'Difficult to tell,' she said, 'but I shouldn't think so.

Even a thug like Boyo started off trying to make it look as if his regime was law-abiding, putting his enemies on trial on a variety of charges. And Basso-Iskani's got the Dangoum conference to think of. It'll be a big thing for him if he can persuade the OAU to go ahead with that. They're sending observers in next week . . .'

'Why these observers not saying to Basso-Iskani "Where be Michael Kagomi? Where be Doctor Agussa? What they gone do wrong?" '

Sophia shook her head. Her smile was tired.

'Maybe they'll ask delicately, in private,' she said. 'The OAU really need the conference to go ahead, you see, if they can get away with it in front of world opinion. Provided Basso-Iskani can keep things quiet, no popular uprisings, no newsworthy massacres, no Europeans or Americans getting hurt . . . that reminds me – you never told me what happened at Tsheba. They're still managing to keep that hushed up.'

Paul began, but his heart wasn't in it. He kept thinking about what the DDA might be doing to Michael to get confessions out of him so that they could put him on trial. Soon Jilli took over, telling the story her way, dancing it, despite being seated in the chair, using her arms and hands and the movements of her long neck to express the explosion of horror among the peaceful farmers of the Strip.

'Hold it,' said Sophia almost at once. 'I'd like to get this on tape.'

She set up a recorder and Jilli started again while Joel filmed her. She'd never seen a tape or a camera before, but she put on a real performance, like Judah acting bible stories at the camp fire, adding details

103

and decorations to the earlier version, living it over. Sophia clapped when she finished.

'Great stuff,' said Joel. 'Let's hope we can get it out of the country. I'll splice it into that stuff about the rock-rabbits, maybe. OK, so what happens next, now you've got this far?'

'Maybe you go take Francis to Papp, along by Shidi?' said Paul. 'This way, Papp knowing you be friends.'

Sophia and Joel looked at each other.

'We'll have to think about it,' said Sophia slowly. 'To be honest, we can't afford taking sides in a situation like this. We're pushing our luck already, leaving Dangoum without a permit to stop some crook of a bureaucrat pinching our truck and gear. If Mr Papp is an enemy of the new regime . . .'

'Papp done finish fighting,' said Paul. 'He hang him AK up into top of old ghost-tree. If Basso-Iskani leaving him alone, no trouble. Only I best say you this. One day Francis go become Prime Minister for Nagala. Michael Kagomi, my father, saying this.'

They laughed, looking down at little Francis lying in his blanket, sleepily nibbling a biscuit.

'OK,' said Joel. 'It's never any harm having a friend or two in high places. We'll take Francis on to Mr Papp. What about you two, then?'

'Going to Dangoum,' said Paul. 'See how for lift Michael Kagomi out from prison.'

'Jeez, you have big ambitions, you Nagala,' said Joel.

'Do you understand what you're saying?' said Sophia.

'You listen,' said Paul. 'Don't you go say this too difficult, too dangerous. I know. I knowing all that.

But I saying to you, what for Michael Kagomi make me him son, if I don't go try for him? Big chance I get killed. Big chance I don't get to do nothing. Little, little chance I do something help my father. But this little chance, this all I see. This be where I must go try and try and try.'

He had spoken quietly, as much to himself as to the others, looking straight out across the bush. Now he nodded emphatically and glanced up.

'Let's hope you make it,' said Sophia. 'I hear he's a very good man, Kagomi.'

Next morning Jilli and Paul stood just below the crest of the next range of hills and watched the truck thread its way back sidelong down the northern slope. In less than two hours Joel had brought them a good three days' march. Over the crest and down lay the railway. Francis's small hand waved from the window of the truck. He had woken feeling fine, and had fallen head over heels in love with Sophia the moment she'd opened her mouth and spoken the kind of English he approved of.

Jilli, it turned out, was equally smitten. As the truck dwindled towards the brown, tree-sprinkled plain she sighed.

'What does Sophia do for work, Paul?'

'She's a journalist.'

'OK. When I get to Dangoum I'll be a journalist too.'

'Take you a bit of time. Much better than being a waitress, if you can make it, though.'

'Waitress! Don't you ever say that word to me again . . . Do you know what a journalist does, Paul?'

# Six

The fire-circle was still there, unmistakable. It had taken Paul a while to find it, looking back across the plain towards the railway and trying to match the view with the one he remembered, when he had lain and kept watch that blazing morning when the war had ended, almost a year ago now. From the fire-circle he found the termites' nest, and from that the rock and the bean-tree. You always buried an arms-cache between three checkpoints, in case one got burnt, or washed away in the rains, or something. The bush might seem unchanging, but nothing in it stayed the same long.

He paced the distances. They didn't match up, and his heart sank till he thought *A whole year – I've grown – I'm stepping longer.* He shortened his paces and found the meeting-point. With his knife and spear-stick he loosened the ground. The rains had softened the surface to slimy clay and then the sun had baked it back hard, hard as the wall of a hut, but as soon as he was through the first couple of inches he could feel that the soil had been disturbed. He hacked it into chunks with his knife and scooped it out with his hands. The deeper he dug the looser the earth became. It should have been back-breaking, bending into the pit in the heat of noon, hacking and scooping, but he had no need to rest. His heart sang with certainty. His hand knew when it could lay the knife aside and probe down through the loosened chunks and touch something different, the smoothness of a plastic sack, the sharp lines of trip-wire binding it round. He stretched out on the scorching earth and lay still, feeling the parcel. It was a moment like an oracle, like a soft voice speaking in his head, telling him that in the whole of enormous Africa he had come to this one spot, these few inches, and found his treasure. *My mother's voice*, he thought. *She is saying that in spite of everything I will lift Michael free.*

He scooped out more soil and worked the parcel loose, then carried it back down the slope to where he had left Jilli on watch, not because he needed a sentry but because he had wanted to be alone. She said nothing as he undid the binding, but took the wire from him and rolled it into a tidy coil. He eased the gun out of the plastic, piece by piece, and wiped the oil from the glistening metal. He unplugged the barrel and assembled the gun, body and barrel, return spring, bolt and bolt-carrier (always tricky to get right, but his fingers remembered every move) and receiver-cover. He wiped the eighteen rounds, fed them into the magazine and clipped it into place. At last he rose, cradling the gun on his right arm, put his feet into the firing stance, raised the butt to his shoulder and sighted towards the distant hills.

Jilli clapped her hands.

'You're a big man now,' she said.

They laughed together.

# Seven

The trail of smoke lay horizontal in the almost windless air, dark, cindery, humped into writhing snake-shapes which slowly lost their outline at the further end while the train puffed fresh hummocks into the scrawl as it took the long curve below the hills. Jilli and Paul had seen it coming for miles. Now they could hear it too.

They lay in a hollow they had scooped at the top of the embankment above the section of double track. The train they could see was bringing empty ore-trucks up from the coast. It would steam into the siding, halt and wait for the other train, laden with ore from the Baroba mines, to pass. Jilli and Paul had watched the procedure yesterday, from the other side, hiding in the nearest patch of uncleared bush, fifty yards away. Boarding the train wasn't going to be nearly as easy as Paul had hoped.

All down the line the bush grew close along the track, but round the siding it had been poisoned and burnt. And though the war was over there were still armed guards on the trains, two men with AKs and two with a big machine-gun. The sides of the ore-trucks were higher than he'd expected, and once inside one you'd find yourself in a sort of giant's cooking-pan under the tropic sun. You wouldn't stay alive in there long. Yesterday's up train had pulled a few goods-wagons behind the ore-trucks, three of them with tarpaulins. If you could get under one of those . . . But they'd been at the rear of the train, almost next to the guard's van, where the machine-gun was set up. The top of the embankment that end was a stony outcrop. There was no hiding there.

Yesterday there had been just one moment when the other train had come through, and the bored men on the waiting train had leaned out and yelled greetings and insults to their friends, and craned further for a while, watching the other guard's van dwindle towards the coast. It would have to be then.

And it would have to be today. Joel had given them a spare flask and they'd brought all the water they could carry, caching most of it while they fetched the AK, but now it was almost gone. There was just about enough to see them through to tomorrow morning.

The train neared. The wail of its whistle drifted through the roasting air. Now they could hear the hammer of iron wheels on the rail-joints. The rhythm slowed, then stopped in the bang-bang-bang of closing buffers. The two Warriors lay still, not raising their heads, knowing that this was a moment of alert, with the soldiers looking around while the fireman climbed down to change the points.

With a fresh whoosh the train came on. The links between the trucks banged taut. The hiss and thud of the pistons and the whump of expelled gases passed below. They smelt the coaly breath, felt the shadow of the smoke pass over, heard another big sigh of steam, ending with the triple wail of the whistle.

Paul counted to a hundred, then lifted his head till he could see along the top of the embankment with his right eye. Nothing. And nothing the other way.

Delicately he peeped further. They had spread the spoil from the hollow they'd made into a low mound which looked flat from any distance, but had left notches in the parapet through which they could see the line below. None of the soldiers yesterday had bothered to climb the embankment. It was mid-afternoon, in the hot season. The war was over.

Directly below stood the line of empty ore-trucks, battered and rusty, the metal of their tall sides seeming to quiver with heat as they absorbed the sun. A soldier was leaning out of the van behind the tender, talking to the fireman. The other way, at the rear of the train, as yesterday, were a few goods-wagons. Only the leading one, which was a flat-top, had a tarpaulin, covering some kind of large crate at the rear and sloping at the front down over something lower and more curved. It might have been a small car. There'd be room in beside it, anyway, for a couple of bodies. If they could get there.

A soldier was examining the lashings on the tarpaulin. As he straightened Paul saw that he was a corporal, in good new fatigues, and wearing a bright purple beret. Paul could see two men at the machine-gun in the open-sided guard's van, so he wasn't one of the regular guards. They were a slovenly lot, anyway.

Now across the silent bush, faint but clear, floated the sound of a whistle. The waiting train answered with a double hoot. Paul's heart began to hammer, as it always did before action. He could feel the adrenalin tingle through his bloodstream. The distant whistle came again, nearer now, and now they could hear the noise of the train itself, pounding steadily on down the slight gradient. Paul nudged Jilli to get ready and heard her answering murmur. The coming train barely slowed. He checked that the sling of the AK was settled on his shoulder over the satchel strap, gripped the handle of the flask and tensed. The next whistle-hoot was almost on top of him. The engine came hammering through.

'Now!' he yelled, rose, and careered down the slope, straight at the nearest truck. Reaching it he turned right and raced along beside the track. The slight curve of the siding meant that the trucks themselves hid him from the soldiers at either end, but the cover narrowed the closer he came. There'd be a stretch where he'd be in view from the guard's van if anyone was looking this way. With two ore-trucks still to go he ducked in under the buffers and started to wriggle his way through.

The bodies of the trucks were slung lower than the axles, sloping down at the centre till they barely cleared the sleepers, but there was just space to squirm through on elbows and knees, after sliding the AK round so that it hung along his chest. He dragged the water-flask through after him. It was slow going. He could hear Jilli, less encumbered, gasping close behind. The noises of the other train were dwindling away. Men's voices were calling. He was halfway through under the last truck when he heard the rattle of points. He wriggled on. The whistle sounded as he rose into the gap in front of the first goods-wagon and slung the flask up on to the loose slope of the tarpaulin. Jilli rose panting beside him. He grabbed her under the arms and lifted her bodily up as the bang of tautening links closed in. Just as the wagon jerked forward he heaved himself up and hung with his belly against the edge of the flat-top and his legs dangling.

111

Jilli hadn't been ready for the acceleration, which sprawled her back on to the slope of the tarpaulin. The water-flask began to slide. He slung a leg up and stopped it with his knee.

'Help! Quick!' he called.

She wriggled herself across and grabbed the handle, then lay there while Paul twisted himself round to perch on the edge of the flat-top. He helped her up to sit beside him. The rails and sleepers swept dizzyingly below. The bush spun past on either side. The wall of the ore-truck in front blasted the sun's heat at them. The wheels hammered deafeningly on the uneven track. Their spines juddered at every rail-joint.

Panting, Paul looked across at Jilli. She'd never done anything like this before, never known this clamour of man-shaped iron or felt such shaking onrush, such obvious danger if she should fall beneath the pounding wheels. He could see she was scared, but still she was laughing with triumph.

'We're going to Dangoum!' she crowed.

Paul laughed too. He gripped the rim of the truck with his left hand, lifted his AK free and raised it overhead in the guerrilla salute.

'Basso-Iskani!' he shouted. 'You'd best watch out! The Warriors are coming to get you!'

The tarpaulin was lashed to cleats round the rim of the flat-top. They untied four along the front and one round the corner and rolled it back till they could slide the satchel and flask and Jilli's roll of clothes and finally themselves into the stifling cavern beneath, but it was harder to fasten it back into place. Even Jilli's supple fingers couldn't manage the last cleat. They couldn't just leave it dangling. The corporal had checked the lashings at the last halt and would probably do so again. Knots don't untie themselves. But things decay quickly in the tropics. The cords were worn and weak. Paul chose one and rubbed it steadily against the edge of the flat-top till it gave, then re-tied the rest. The loose section also meant that they could prop the rim of the tarpaulin up with the butt of the AK to scoop a draught of air through into the darkness.

What next? Paul lay on the oily timber and tried to think. 'Just after you've hit your target,' Michael once said, 'that's a big danger-point. Don't sit down and rest. Nine times out of ten there'll be someone or something looking for a chance to hit back at you.' The loose lashing was a worry. Maybe the corporal would just re-tie it, but maybe he'd look in underneath. Paul touched Jilli's shoulder.

'Just going to explore,' he said.

The load at the front of the wagon turned out to be a car. The hot dark reeked of newness, new rubber, new paint, new plastic, fresh, clean oil. In the faint light from the airhole Paul caught the glimmer of chrome on the radiator, the three-pointed Mercedes symbol he'd seen on the limousine in which Michael had fetched him from Tsheba. But this was something much smaller. Crawling along by its flank he found it was a two-seater convertible, the sort he'd seen film stars driving sometimes in pictures in magazines. You had to be rich to own a toy like this. The Minister of Commerce, the one who'd given his son the helicopter, perhaps he'd ordered this for his daughter. Before the coup, that would have been. No. There was a soldier looking after it, a corporal, so it must be for

113

someone still in power. What did it matter? Provided it gave Paul and Jilli somewhere to hide.

Under the car? Its clearance was less than five inches. (What a toy for Nagala! There couldn't be twenty miles of road where you could risk driving it!)

In it, then? The roof was down and the seat-cover in place, fastened with pops too stiff to move. Ah, there was a zip down the centre. Paul eased it back and found he could loose the pops. Could he fasten it all back from inside? Lying across the front seat he experimented. Yes – pops first, then zip, easing the fastener up the last few inches with the tip of his knife. The result was a suffocating pit.

He undid the fastenings and told Jilli what he'd found. They stowed their stores in the car, keeping only the flask to drink from, then did five practice runs till they had the drill right. After that they rested, dozing by the draught of air, though they got a couple more practices when the train slowed almost to walking pace before picking up speed again.

Third time was for real. By now it was night, and cooler. Paul was dreaming, and at first the changing wheel-rhythm was part of his dream, but then Jilli was pinching his arm and he was awake. She took the flask. He eased the AK clear, checked that the worn tie was dangling outside the canvas, and followed her round. Now the wheel-hammer had a new, booming note as the train moved on at a walking-pace. Jilli wriggled herself into the slot behind the seats.

'What's that noise?' she whispered.

'Bridge over the Oloro, I think. Malani tried to blow it up a couple of years back and they're still repairing it. There'll be a bridge-guard, for sure, but maybe they won't stop an ore-train.'

114

The wheel-hammer dulled, marking where the bridge ended, but the train loitered only a few more clacks and stopped. Paul lay in the utter dark, breathing shallow and slow to use as little oxygen as possible. Time oozed by, but much of his life had consisted of this sort of wary waiting. Lucky it was night, he thought. Lie here this long in full sun and you'd be dead of heat-stroke.

At last he heard voices, not orders or arguments, just talk. They came slowly nearer, interrupted by pauses and grunts. Two men, checking the trucks, by the sound of it. For stowaways, maybe. Now they were near enough for him to hear that they were discussing something that had happened in a local football match. They reached the flat-top and began to loosen the tarpaulin. The loose tie didn't bother them. He heard a flop and scrape as they folded a section back. They'd have a hand torch, of course.

'Ho!' said a voice. 'Somebody's going to give his girl a good time!'

'Get up and see how she feels to drive?'

A mumble of doubt. Paul reached for the AK and laid it along his thighs with his finger on the trigger-guard. He could take one man for sure, the second probably. The other soldiers would be half asleep. Good chance of making a run for it.

The men were loosing more lashings when a new voice shouted, from a distance.

'Hey! You leave that truck alone!'

'Just checking, man. Just checking.'

Approaching boots scrunched on loose track-ballast.

'Don't you touch this car. It's evidence for the trials.'

'Then the old judge gets to keep it, uh?'

'No damn judge. General Basso-Iskani sent me personally to Jom-jom, just to bring it back safe. So you put that tarpaulin right back on. There's nothing in under there. I've had my eye on it all up from the coast.'

'OK, OK. What about these trials, then?'

'Soon as they get to confess.'

'You palace guard, man?'

'Right. Don't you see my cap? You better watch it, fellow. We don't bother getting confessions out of the likes of you.'

The first two laughed uncertainly, as if knowing it was only half a joke. The tarpaulin scraped. Their voices returned to football as they re-tied the lashings and moved away. At last the whistle sounded, the engine whumped steam and the links banged taut. The train gathered speed and clacked on. Paul slid the zip open and helped Jilli out. All the ties were fastened now, but threads of night air whispered through the eye holes where the ties held the canvas. Paul lay on the rough deck dozing and waking. The wheel-judder drummed through his dreams, the same images coming back and back, him here, on this train, but running now into a black tunnel and then out into a faint-lit track along a corridor with steel doors either side. Fingers, bloody and broken, gripped the bars of the grilles. On some of the doors was a large black check-mark – that meant the prisoner had confessed. Paul had the key to Michael's cell in his satchel, if only he could find it among the spent cartridge-cases, if only the train would stop . . . and then the wheels in his dream would slow and he would prepare to leap, but leap instead into waking, and know where he was, still drumming through the bush towards Dangoum.

And then he woke and saw daylight spearing through the eyelets. The train was back to a walking-pace and the track seemed very bad. Peeping through an eyelet he glimpsed thin bush. It was about a hundred miles from the Oloro to Dangoum, he remembered, but they hadn't even reached the Flats yet. He dozed again, and next time he woke they were going a little faster, and now through the eyelet he could see grey-white desert reeling by.

'Not far now,' he said. 'An hour, maybe two.'

'How'll we get off the train, Paul?'

'Have to wait and see.'

It was the next big problem, with the truck being closely watched by the corporal from the palace guard. The AK made it worse. Without that they could have been just another couple of kids stowing away to reach the shanty towns in the forlorn hope of a better life, and got off with nothing worse than kicks and buffets. With it they were something else. Besides, there'd been an amnesty under Malani, when all weapons were supposed to have been handed in. Now it was a crime to carry one. He'd have to make some kind of parcel, disguising its shape. What with? Jilli's grass mats might have done, but they'd left them all but one up in those dreadful hills. One wasn't enough. Something out of the car, then? Yes.

He crawled round, climbed in and carefully slit round the leather of the seat-covers with his knife. Beneath the leather was a layer of cloth. Perfect. He cut it free in big patches. Too soon to make the parcel, though – he might need the gun still. Wait till the last minute. But Basso-Iskani was going to have a nasty surprise when he unzipped the cover of his nice new car! He could send for fresh seats, of course. Pity . . .

Meditatively Paul's fingers caressed the exposed chair-stuffing. Why not destroy the car? Completely. That would be better still. The anger of his dream still bubbled like vomit in his throat. Yes. Get rid of Basso-Iskani's car. If it was really wanted for evidence at a trial, that might delay the trial, help Michael somehow. If it was just coming up for Basso-Iskani to play with, it would still be a blow at the enemy. It was going to hurt. Good.

He understood his own feelings better than he might have. During the winter offensive two years back the commando had mined a road and lain in ambush, waiting for the soldiers who used it, but then the army trucks had come past behind a battered old pick-up driven by a farmer. The soldiers kept their guns on him, forcing him to follow the road. A boy, his son probably, sat beside him. His wheel had gone over the mine. Paul had seen the boy's body twisting through the air, his arms spread wide as though he had learnt to fly. The trucks had swung round the wreckage and roared on. Michael had talked to the Warriors about it that night.

'Don't tell yourselves it is only one of those things that happens in a war. Don't argue this way – we have right and justice on our side, so we must act, we must fight. This is true, but the next part of the argument is false. We are right, but that doesn't make everything we do right also. It wasn't right for this man and this boy to die. When your enemies are strong and you are weak you mustn't say to yourself "I cannot striked them directly, so I will strike elsewhere".

118

Next step after that you'll be putting car-bombs into crowded markets and burning villages whose people are too scared to help you and executing foreign aid workers. And soon the rightness that was on your side is dead. It could no longer breathe, because it was smothered by the wrongness of the things you did for its sake.'

But I will strike at my enemy, thought Paul. Basso-Iskani has Michael in his prisons, and this is his car. I will show him he hasn't won yet.

Justin had given the Warriors a lesson in how to destroy army trucks, using their own fuel, or a petrol bomb if they were diesel-powered. No bottle. Petrol, though, maybe. He crawled out round the flank of the car and found the filler-cap by touch. It wasn't locked. Fumes reeked out into the stifling air. That would explode all right! But he'd need a good long fuse. What? Aha!

He crawled forward to where Jilli lay peering through one of the eyelets.

'Look, Paul,' she said. 'Fields, like the Strip!'

Paul peered. She was right. Dusty green fields stretched away. Farmers hoed and ploughed and carried water on shoulder-yokes. The train must be passing through the ring of irrigated land, fed by the water from the aquifer, that surrounded Dangoum.

'We'll be getting there soon, Jilli. Put on your town clothes. And can I have your grass belt, please?'

'What for?'

'Blow up Basso-Iskani's car. Boom!'

He grinned at the thought.

'Ah, the car's too pretty!'

But she unwound the belt and gave it to him. It was just what he needed, a half-inch ribbon of plaited grass, bone dry and about five feet long. He crawled back, unfastened the filler-cap and fed one end of the belt down into the tank as far as it would go. When he pulled it out it was reeking wet. He did the same with the other and replaced the filler-cap – it was too risky to allow an explosive mixture to build up under the canvas, or the car would explode as soon as he lit a match. Carefully he pinched the belt double all down its length and opened it out into a V-section, so that when he laid it along the timber beside the rear wheel and the crate behind it didn't lie flat. Then he crawled to the front again, unclipped the magazine of the AK and folded the butt, and rolled them up in the leather from the car-seats, wrapping the strips of cloth round the parcel and tying them loosely in place. Mentally he rehearsed the moves he'd need to cut the cord, assemble the gun and fire. About eight seconds, he thought.

'OK,' he said. 'Come along back. You bring the flask.'

Carrying the satchel in his teeth and cradling the AK he led the way to the rear. Once there he took out the matches and laid them ready, with the butt of one protruding from the box, then stacked flask, gun and satchel against the back of the crate. With his knife he slit the tarpaulin almost from side to side, just above the line of the eyelets. The train wasn't going fast enough to make it flap, and the taller truck behind hid the slit from the guard's van.

He raised the canvas and they peered out. There was a road now, running beside the track, with a few shacks and a dump of wrecked cars through which children roamed. An air-liner climbed into the sky beyond, so the airport must be over there. About two miles to go now. Next time the train stopped they'd make a run for it.

'OK,' he said. 'Be ready. When I say "Go" you get out, quick as you can. I'll pass you the gun. You put it on the ground. I'll give you the flask and the satchel and you take them back under this next truck, quick as you can. Wait for me by the back wheels. OK?'

She touched the gun-parcel, flask and satchel in turn, and nodded. There were shanties now beside the track, with only a chain-link fence, rusted and broken in many places, to keep them from spilling on to the railway. Rubbish littered the railside. Kites probed and squabbled. If only the train would stop here, it would be easy. Twice it seemed to be slowing and Paul tensed for action before it picked up speed again. And now there were rusty, broken sheds and shabby breeze-block buildings, and a few sidings.

The train slowed, whistled, slowed to a crawl. The bang of closing buffers began.

Paul wriggled along by the crate, undid the filler-cap, laid the end of the belt into the pipe and wedged it in place with the little grass apron. The flat-top jarred to a halt as he twisted back.

'Go!' he shouted. 'Go!'

Jilli was out by the time he reached the corner of the crate, her hand groping through the slit. He passed her the gun, then the satchel and flask, wriggled back round the corner again, picked up the matches, struck one and laid it against the belt. Blue and yellow, the flame moved away, dazzling in that dark.

He flung himself backwards, twisted at the corner and dived head first through the slit, grabbing the hook of the further truck and tucking his knees up to swing himself down through the gap. The gun was laid ready. He snatched it, still in the momentum of his rush, and ducked in under the next wagon. Jilli was there, crouched by the further axle. As he wriggled beneath the near one the car went up.

It exploded with a soft, enormous whoosh. Heat crackled along either side of the track. Yellow tussocks went suddenly black, the flame of their burning invisible in the sunlight. The reflected heat blasted roasting in under the shelter of the truck, then passed on.

'Quick! Quick!' Paul snapped, gesturing with his free hand.

At once Jilli was twisting beneath the axle, ducking across the slot of sunlight between the trucks and in under the next one. Legs appeared in the open, men jumping from the guard's van. There were yells. She froze. Paul slipped across the gap and crouched in the shadow beside her. The legs ran past, three pairs in khaki fatigues and one in jeans, all on the left of the train. Paul twisted and looked the other way. A shed of some kind, a breeze-block wall and the bottom of a broken window, only a few feet from the track.

'This way!'

He scuttled into the open, rose and dashed along beside the wall. The heat of burning smote at his shoulders. He whipped round the corner of the shed and on round the next corner, then stood with his back against the wall, with the gun-parcel in his left hand and his knife poised to cut the cords. A scamper of feet and Jilli was at his side with the satchel and flask.

A few yards away stood a lorry, its axles propped on blocks and all four wheels missing. The door hung open, half off its hinges. Paul pointed and at once Jilli was across the gap and wriggling up. He followed. The windscreen was broken. Crouching in front of the seat they peered through the cracked glass. Men came pouring out of sheds in ragged working clothes, mostly bare-footed. They stared for a moment at the blazing wagon and ran towards it. Soldiers appeared round a corner, half a dozen of them, with AKs. They too stared and ran. The last stragglers went by.

'OK,' said Paul. 'Let's go.'

He slid down and waited, clutching the gun parcel under his arm. She passed him the satchel and followed.

'Don't hurry,' he said.

'Let's make like we're sweethearts,' said Jilli, twining her fingers into his. She laid her head against his shoulder and giggled as they strolled away. At the corner round which the soldiers had come Paul risked a glance back. The car and the crate behind it were both ablaze, and the box-wagon beyond was burning too. A ring of soldiers and onlookers watched from a safe distance. Jilli sighed.

'You're my friend, Paul?'

'Sure.'

'You'll be a big man, one day. A big man in the government. Then you'll buy me a pretty car like that one?'

# Eight

Behind them in the railway yard something exploded, followed by screams and yells, but there was no pursuit, and the road ahead was as empty and silent as the bush. They trudged through the roasting grey dust, between storehouses and workshops which had been built near the railway years ago, when trade had been good, but were now mostly broken and boarded up. The reek of heated metal blasted from one open doorway, but the men who'd been working there were now settling into bits of shade for their midday rest. None of them glanced at the passers-by.

Rubbish lay in drifts around the buildings. A burnt-out pick-up nuzzled into a wall – it must have tried to take a corner too fast. Paul had seen pick-ups like that careering round Dangoum on his previous visit, crammed with illegal fare-paying passengers. This one had been battered and patched many times before its final crash, and one of the patches was a strip of corrugated iron, now almost loose. Paul wrenched it free, bent it double and slotted the parcel with the gun in it into the fold, tying it firm with the last of his cord.

'Best if I carry it,' said Jilli.

She made a pad with his spare shirt and he helped her balance the awkward load on her head, then took the flask and walked beside her.

'You look fine,' he said. 'We're just another couple

of people who've made it to Dangoum to look for money.'

Jilli stopped in her tracks and gazed at the desolate, sun-blasted road between the abandoned sheds. A three-legged dog was sniffing the skeleton of a mule for scraps the kites had missed.

'You mean this is *Dangoum?*' she whispered.

Paul grinned at her, Dangoum would be as full of dangers as the bush – fuller, because he didn't yet know its tracks or odours or places of safety, but he felt quite confident, in control. The burning of the Mercedes was a sign to him, not just because he'd made it work and struck a blow at his enemy, but because it had turned out the best thing he could have done. Without that diversion, how would they have got clear of the train and the railway yard? It was as though there had been something helping him, putting the car on that very train, then putting the idea of destruction into his mind. No, not something, someone. *My mother, the war. She loves me still. She is on my side.*

'It's not all like this,' he said. 'The market's the best bit – I'll show you that, and the Hilton, and Boyo's palace. But first I've got to find my friends, OK?'

They trudged on, sweating. The road narrowed till it was almost blocked in places by the shacks and shanties propped against the walls of old sheds. Round the railway the air had smelt mainly of coal and ash and acids. Here it smelt of people. Soon the real shanty town began. A few women and children, listless with heat, moved around, but the men lay like dead bodies in any shade they could find. The burning air was filled with the stenches of cooking and rot and dung, though the downright sun dried any filth it could reach hard and harmless in a couple of hours, and the kites carried away whatever they could eat. Last time he'd come to the shanties Peter had told him he was lucky not to be seeing them in the rains, when the spaces between the huts became a marsh of puddled mud and death was something you could smell in the steamy air. Even now, despite the occasional thump and wail of a radio the shanties seemed like hell, hopeless and helpless. It's a bad time of day, Paul thought. Maybe they'll come alive in the evening.

He walked in front, because that was what a man would do. Nobody looked at them. They were normal – another couple of kids who'd made it across the Flats and were collecting scraps of things they could build a shack with.

The path widened, making space for a small local market, not even stalls, just baskets on the ground with shade-brollies above – a woman with two wizened cockerels in a coop, a boy with a mug and water-jar, a woman with a pile of orange beans, another with slices of water-melon, another with shrivelled black bananas. They looked as if they'd sat there since the last rains, with no one coming to buy anything. A man with one arm was stirring a pot over a fire.

'What've you got in there?' said Paul.

The man spooned a ladle up and let the stuff slop back. It was mealie-porridge, flavoured with a few herbs.

'How much?' said Paul.

'Two gurai a ladle.'

'Pay you three for two.'

'Let's see your money.'

126

Paul produced a five-gura note and his cooking-pan and the man spooned the stuff in. Another gura bought two mugs of water. He settled with Jilli in the shade of the one-armed man's brolly to eat the porridge with his fingers. He was very hungry.

'Pretty good,' he mumbled through porridge.

'Better than we used to eat in the bush,' said the man.

'That where you lost your arm?'

'Bullet through my elbow. Doctor in Shidi cut the rest off.'

Paul grunted understanding. If he'd been in Shidi the man was probably from one of Malani's commandos. Better not say anything yet, though a contact like that might be useful later.

'How did you get yourself money?' said the man.

'My uncle found a dead elephant.'

'There's some born lucky . . . Your girl's Fulu, right? And your uncle said No so you nicked some of his elephant money and cleared out?'

The woman with the bananas cackled and started to pass the joke on to the woman with the beans. Finding a dead elephant was a way of talking. If you were a poacher you shot your elephant and it fell down so you had to go and find it, and of course it was dead by then. You cut off the tusks and sold them to a dealer. A good pair was worth a year's wages. Paul had thought the story out on the train, in case.

'Where's the next stand-pipe?' he said.

'Up along that way. Bear right at the booze-shop. Get a move on, or they'll have closed – or maybe it won't, because the Red Scorpions beat the Death-singers up a couple of nights back and they'll be wanting to show us they're good guys. It'll still cost you a couple of gura, though.'

'I thought it was supposed to be free.'

'Try telling the Scorpions.'

Paul thanked him and moved on. As they passed the bar the porridge-seller had mentioned a man came staggering out, yelling, his face streaming with blood from a knife-slash over his eye. The stand-pipe had a queue waiting, patient in spite of the sweltering sun. One man was working the tap, another taking the money and a third looking on. All three wore T-shirts, jeans and sneakers, but also army berets and leather belts from which hung savage-looking knives. They had long black faces like Kashka's, and their foreheads were smeared with a scarlet squiggle which might have been a scorpion. They spoke to each other in Baroba. They took no special notice of Paul as he paid his money, filled his flask, and carried it back to where Jilli was sitting on the bundle containing the AK. He was impressed, but not frightened. He'd known that Dangoum would have its dangers, like the bush. These were some of its lions.

'I'm tired,' said Jilli.

'Keep going. We'll find you some friends in the market. This way, it should be.'

Paul's mental map of Dangoum was not as detailed as his one of Nagala, but it had a few fixed points. The railway line had come past the airport – he knew where that was – but had then, judging by the swing of the shadows, run north before turning east again to reach the railway yard. Since then they'd come about a mile south, so the down-town towers should be over on their left, with the market roughly half-left. He headed that way until he heard the distant thud of drums from big loudspeakers. Then all he had to do was follow the sound.

Most of the stalls had closed down till the evening, with the stall-holders sleeping beside or beneath them, but the music still roofed the whole space over with noise. Paul moved along the edge to get his bearings. They had come out of the shanties in an area occupied by patchers and menders. Just opposite them a man was finishing a solder job on an old radio. Next door were a couple of bike-repair stalls, beyond that a smithy where the heat of a charcoal furnace still blasted out while three naked men, glistening with sweat, lay in the shade furthest from it. Then a pyramid of used batteries which an old woman employed children to cut apart to extract the lead. Then several stalls which cobbled crude shoes out of worn tyres. Now he knew where he was, and headed in, making for the coppersmiths' area.

Their hammers were silent now, but they were a good landmark. Paul had become interested in them on his earlier visit because they managed to do things their own way, despite being part of the market. They all came from one small tribe in the east and had been copper-workers for generations. They were small, dark people, very proud and independent, who could mend anything copper but also made huge round copper bowls, which in the old days used to be given to great chiefs to show how important they were. They had their own priest in the market, blind and old, but when the two boys who looked after him banged his big copper gong all the smiths would stop what they were doing and come and see what he wanted.

They were resting for the afternoon, like everyone else, but Paul led Jilli past them and on past several stalls where tall women from the far south, with black gum-rings in their hair, sold gaudy blankets, to the area he'd been looking for.

'Yeh!' squeaked Jilli. 'They're Fulu!'

As fast as her load would let her she headed for the nearest stall, where a woman was sitting, resting her back against a stack of large round baskets. She was obviously Fulu, with her pale skin, small bones and hair in a top-knot, though she wore an ordinary T-shirt and a green wrap-around skirt. She twittered an answer to Jilli's question and pointed. Jilli thanked her and stalked off to a stall which sold boat-shaped head-baskets. Here the stall-holder was already lying down, but can't quite have gone to sleep yet, as she sat up when Jilli spoke to her, then rose and took Jilli by the shoulders and stared at her. Jilli, clearly surprised, fell silent. The woman spoke. Paul could hear the sorrow in her voice. Jilli's look of eager greeting changed. She swayed and let go of her load, but Paul managed to catch it as it fell and lower it to the ground. She sat down, put her head in her hands and moaned, rocking to and fro. The woman, crouching beside her with an arm round her shoulders, looked up at Paul.

'You're from Tsheba?' she said.

'Best not tell anyone.'

'Sure. But I'm . . .' she paused to think it out in Naga '. . . Jilli's mother's cousin's husband's cousin's wife. My name's Efoni Doli. I'm part of her long family. I heard the soldiers had killed her with the others.'

'What others?'

'Everyone in her father's house. They waited for her

130

brothers and sisters to come back from the buffalo-pound and shot them too.'

Paul stood, nodding slowly, while he drew a long, sick breath. War was like that. You thought you were used to it, you could see the worst it could do and not flinch, but then it took people who were nothing to do with it, hard-working farmers, a blind old grandmother . . . My mother, the war . . .

'We saw them burning the huts while we were getting away. They were looking for me and Francis and Kashka, I guess. I'm sorry.'

She sighed. Her eye fell on the bundle Jilli had been carrying. Catching it as it fell Paul had let the cloth-wrapped parcel inside slither partly into view.

'What have you got in there?' said Efoni.

'Better not ask. We weren't far from where I'd buried it when the war ended, so I went and dug it up. There's somebody in Dangoum I've got to try and help.'

'Nothing to do with me. We don't want any of that in the market. You'll have to get it out of here.'

Paul looked at her, not understanding. Soldiers had come to the Strip and slaughtered a whole section of what she called her long family, and she thought fighting the government that had sent them wasn't anything to do with her. There was no point in arguing.

'OK,' he said. 'I've got some friends in the Old Town, but I don't know if they're still all right. Mind if I leave Jilli and my other stuff here while I go and check?'

'Sure. You can leave that too for a bit. Shove it in under the baskets. I just want to be sure you know the score. It'll be OK till this evening.'

131

'My thanks.'

He tried to explain to Jilli where he was going, but she didn't seem to hear him, so he took a long drink from the flask and moved off. He didn't want to ask the way to Curzon Street – the less you told anyone the better – but there was a tourist office downtown with a map of Dangoum in its window, so he headed for the nearest of the wide avenues that radiated out from the palace.

Apart from the flies over the piles of rubbish all Dangoum seemed asleep now. The houses of the Old Town, windowless and blind on their street facades, were silent, except for the occasional radio wailing in a dark inner courtyard. The heat was heavy and list-less, more exhausting than the clean heat of the bush. Out in the avenue sleepers sprawled under the palms while the flies hazed over them or crawled across their skins as though they were rubbish too. For block after block Paul trudged on, not seeing a wak-ing soul. Who was using Michael's flat now, he wondered, with its air-conditioning, and the stacked cold Coke in the fridge?

Three blocks from the palace he heard a wailing noise behind him, an up-and-down note coming rapidly nearer. Far down the avenue pale discs were shining through a cloud of dust, headlights, motor-cyclists and cars rushing towards him. The procession swept past, outriders with sirens screaming, a light truck full of soldiers in purple berets, a long black limousine with a flag on its bonnet and blind polar-ized windows – it might have been the very one in which Michael had fetched Paul from Tsheba. Then a second truck full of soldiers, their weapons up and ready. Lashed to its mudguard was the body of a man. The dangling arm bore a corporal's stripes. The lolling head was bare, its black curls soaked with blood. Paul had seen bodies like that before in villages where government soldiers had come through, picking out men at random and 'executing' them. The corporal had been shot at close range in the back of the head.

By Basso-Iskani himself? Gone down to collect his new toy? The railyard must be back that way. There was a corporal he'd sent to Jom-jom with orders to bring the car back safe, one of his own palace guard . . .

Inwardly Paul shrugged. The corporal had boasted to the bridge-guard about getting confessions out of the prisoners. He was enemy. His death was an accident, but he wasn't like the farmer's son who'd been killed when the mine blew up. He had chosen sides. Chosen wrong.

The procession slowed to twist through the gap between a double rampart of sandbags that crossed the avenue a couple of hundred yards short of the palace. Road-block. That hadn't been there on Paul's previous visit. The guard, alerted by the sirens, turned out to salute the limousine. Paul was out of the Old Town now, moving up the roasting canyon between the high-rises at the centre of Dangoum. The tourist office was over to his right, he thought, two radial spokes away, so he turned along one of the connecting side-streets to work his way round. Another road-block had been built across the next avenue, and two soldiers were asleep in the strip of shadow cast by the sandbags. The road-block on the next avenue was incomplete and unguarded. He walked past it and found the tourist office.

It was closed, and by the pile of rubbish in the doorway looked as if it had been like that for a couple of weeks, at least, but the map was still in the dusty window. Curzon Street turned out to be the avenue he had just crossed. Now that he was past the road-blocks the temptation was to go on up to the palace and at least do a recce, see if he could spot some weakness, some culvert, the pipe that fed the moat, perhaps, where he could creep in with his AK . . . It was nonsense, a fantasy, he knew that. As Sophia had said, the chances were that Michael was being held somewhere else, in one of the DDA secret prisons, not in the palace at all, but the dream Paul had had on the train came strongly back into his mind, the bleeding hands on the door-grilles, the dim lights of the pumping hall . . .

What could one boy do, with an old gun and eighteen rounds? You'd need friends, allies, thirty or forty men working together in a surprise attack, explosives to blast your way in . . . And meanwhile Michael was lying somewhere in the stinking dark, listening to the moans from nearby cells, waiting for the torturers' return.

Enough of dreaming! That was no help. Paul turned back past the unfinished road-block, walked on a hundred yards, took a side street and came out into Curzon Street well down from the road-block where the soldiers slept. The address Michael had left in the package with the money had been 300, but few of the houses had numbers. He needn't have worried. 300 had been some kind of bar, and the owner had been proud enough of his number to paint it in enormous yellow figures across the front of the building. But it was shut – not just shut through the midday heat but shut for good. The door had been smashed in and roughly boarded across. The nail-heads in the planks gleamed rustless, so they'd not been there long. There was no sound or light from behind the broken door, no windows on the street. Paul turned away and walked on. He didn't like the look of it. Best thing would be to carry on a couple of blocks and then work round and up the other side of Curzon Street. He could lie in the shade under one of the palms and pretend to be asleep while he watched.

Forty yards on a car was parked, a green saloon which had looked empty, but as Paul got nearer turned out to have a man in it, lolling in the back seat, apparently asleep, though he was wearing dark glasses which made it hard to tell. As Paul was about to pass he sat up, opened the door and slid out. He was tall and thin, his skin purply-black like Kashka's, though he didn't otherwise look Baroba. He wore a pale fawn suit with a clean white T-shirt beneath the jacket.

'You,' he said.

'Please?' said Paul.

'What are you after?'

'Find a place I can get a drink. They said there was a bar down this way.'

'Closed down. Come over here.'

Paul put his hand to his belt and stayed where he was. At the man's first step towards him he drew his knife. The man stopped, slid a hand into his jacket pocket and produced a cylinder of black wood. He flipped a catch and a lean blade shot up. He smiled.

'Makes two of us,' he said. 'Where did you steal yours?'

'Fought another boy for it. He took it off a dead soldier.'

'Uh huh. You'd need cash for a drink.'

'Sure.'

'Let's see it.'

Paul shook his head. The man hesitated. If they fought he'd win, of course, but Paul might get a thrust in and he had his sharp fawn suit to think of. He slid the blade slowly back into its handle and put the knife away. Paul lowered his guard.

'OK,' said the man. 'Too hot for work. But you can clear out and not come back, not unless you want the Deathsingers paying you a visit.'

'I just want a drink.'

'Find a stand-pipe,' said the man wearily, and turned back to the car.

Paul made his way back to the market by side streets, feeling deeply depressed. Michael's safe house had been raided, and was still being watched, watched by a man who had something to do with the Deathsingers – Michael told him they had worked with the secret police, the DDA. The man in the fawn suit might be from the DDA. Sophia had said the DDA were probably holding Michael and the other prisoners. It was all very, very bad.

He found the market coming to life. Customers were moving between the stalls. The voices of traders – calling wares, haggling, mocking competitors – wove in with the drumbeat from the sound system. As he approached the Fulu section the clatter of the coppersmith's hammers drowned out most other sounds. Efoni was rearranging her baskets.

'You find your friends?'

He shook his head. She looked displeased but said no more. Jilli had pulled herself together from her grief, buried it somehow inside herself, and was sitting cross-legged by a sheaf of reeds beginning to weave something. He squatted down beside her.

'Jilli, I'm sorry. All this happened because you helped me.'

She looked at him, her small head poised proudly on her long neck.

'I'm a Warrior,' she said. 'Now I know what that means. I know why I'm a Warrior. Same as you, Paul.'

He nodded and stroked the back of her hand with his fingertips. It was worse for her, different. He never thought about his own family, or what had happened to them. He couldn't remember any of that. Jilli could never forget.

'What are you making?' he said.

'Basket for your gun – like a head-basket, only longer. You can buy some cottons to hide it. I've seen a lot of people walking around like that.'

Paul had too. The narrow Fulu head-baskets were popular in Dangoum. Mostly you saw women carrying them, but men and boys too. There'd be nothing odd about a boy with a basket containing a few rolls of cloth.

'My thanks,' he said. 'That'll be just right – Efoni told me to get my gun out of the market. I've got a problem, Jilli. The house my father told me to go to – it's boarded up, and there's a man watching it, from the DDA, I think. That's the secret police. They're bad. I don't know what to do next. Efoni said she didn't want me here.'

'Oh, she can't say that! I'll talk to her!'

Jilli jumped to her feet, and went off to argue with Efoni. Paul swigged some water and tried to think. He wasn't really bothered about shelter – it was the

137

dry season and he could sleep in the open. He had plenty of money for food. Jilli seemed to have solved the problem of the AK. All that was unimportant – what mattered was helping Michael. There was no way he could do that alone, so he had to find allies. Who? There must be other people in Dangoum, lots of them, who had supported Malani and would fight again if they got the chance. Surely there must be groups and cells already planning revolt. How could he find them, join them? Perhaps the one-armed man who'd sold him the porridge might have a contact – he'd been a Malani fighter . . .

Efoni came round the pile of baskets shaking her head, but smiling.

'Jilli says I've got to keep you on,' she said. 'Won't take No for an answer.'

'My thanks. What about that?'

Paul jerked his head to where the gun was tucked away.

'Provided you get it good and hidden, and don't go waving it round. OK, you can sleep here – at least it means I don't have to carry the whole lot home every night. Jilli can sleep in my hut, but I haven't got room for you. OK?'

'That's fine. My thanks, Efoni. Anything I can do?'

'You can go and fill my water-jug if you like. The stand-pipe's down by the music-trees.'

'How much to pay?'

'Still free in the market. There'll be trouble if anyone tries to change that.'

Efoni and Jilli left a bit before midnight, each stalking off under a tower of Efoni's best baskets and moving away between the butane flares that lit the stalls.

Tired though he was after the effort of the last two days and the almost sleepless nights between, Paul stayed awake another hour, digging a shallow pit at the back of the stall with his knife, laying the AK in it, smoothing it over and covering the place with a pile of baskets. Then he slept.

The market stayed noisy all night. Though the big speakers went off at midnight there were liquor stalls at the further side, where the prostitutes came and went, and smaller sound systems played on, and voices rose in singing and quarrel. The habits of the bush kept Paul sleeping light as a deer. If footsteps strayed up from the liquor stalls he would be instantly awake, with his hand stretched out under the baskets ready to push down through the loosened earth to the AK. And he was aware of its presence even in his dream, the same dream coming and going, himself not on the train now but crawling up some kind of water-tunnel with the gun slung beneath him, then looking out into a room where a band was playing, tall thin men in T-shirts with notes of music on them. Cells round the room, the grilles, the blood-stained fingers. The whole attack timed, Kashka and the Leopards ready to set their mine off against the far wall of the palace, and then the lights would go out and Paul would dash from his hiding-place and slide the gun through the bars of Michael's grille . . . if he could work out which one it was, if the man in the fawn suit, knowing about the attack all along, hadn't begun to turn the big wheel which would let the water come roaring out of the sluices and wash him, drowning, down into darkness . . .

A bad night.

Efoni and Jilli came soon after dawn, bringing him

139

breakfast, black beans with a few shreds of chicken for flavour. He thanked them, told Efoni what he'd done about the gun, and left. He'd have liked Jilli to come too. She'd said nothing more to him about the massacre of her family, but he could sense her grief and desolation. In the war you learnt about things like that, the strange guilt survivors feel, when all their friends have perished. Helping him look for allies against Basso-Iskani might have put fresh images into her mind. But it turned out she was determined to finish the basket to hide the AK. Well, perhaps, he thought, choosing the cottons to cover it might help in a different way. He gave her some money and left.

The one-armed porridge-seller was no use. He just shook his head and said those times were over. No, he didn't know anyone.

Paul turned away sighing. What now? His mind was still full of his dream. The idea of the palace seemed to call to him. Maybe Michael wasn't there. Maybe there wasn't a water-tunnel, or anything like one, though the moat must be fed somehow. But at least he could go and watch. He might learn something.

This time he made his way up by a different route, deliberately choosing the road that would take him past Michael's flat. He walked steadily at first but long before he reached the downtown towers began to mooch and loiter, gazing into shop windows, or standing and staring when the occasional sleek Mercedes purred by. He was a boy in a big city, loafing around because he had nothing better to do.

Nothing better to do than stand for a while outside Michael's apartment block watching who came and went. If Peter showed up he would follow him, but he didn't. The one interesting thing he saw was a cream-coloured convertible driven by a fat middle-aged man smoking a cigar. Two young women in expensive-looking clothes sat beside him, laughing and waving their arms about. When the car stopped the women kissed the man, got out and strutted into the building on high-heeled shoes, still giggling and showing themselves off. The man gazed around with a grand, self-pleased look, noticed Paul and tossed his half-smoked cigar in his direction. Paul pounced and grinned his thanks, as he was expected to, and the man drove on.

Soldiers were working at another uncompleted road-block at the top of the avenue. Paul strolled towards them, scuffing a bit of melon-slice along the ground and glancing up casually to see if there was an unwatched gap where he might slip through. It took him a moment or two to realize that the men were not building the road-block, but demolishing it, loading sandbags and poles into trucks which then drove away. A soldier with an AK was lounging under a palm-tree, watching. Paul had never seen a man look so bored, but as Paul scuffled his bit of melon past the remains of the barrier he glanced round.

'Where are you going, son?'

'My grandad told me to come and look at the palace. He said I'd got to build him a house like that.'

'Hopeful. What've you got there?'

'Bit of cigar a man gave me to show how rich he was. Do you want it?'

'Sure. Thanks. Got a light?'

Paul got the matches out of his satchel and passed them over. The soldier lit the cigar butt and sucked

141

the smoke luxuriously in. He didn't give the matches back, of course, but he looked fairly friendly.

'What are they doing?' said Paul.

'Don't ask me. Put it up last week, take it down this – that's the army.'

'Can I go and look at the palace?'

The soldier shrugged, and Paul mooched on.

The broad road that ringed the palace was called the Circus. On its outer side the pavement was shaded all the way round by a double row of acacia trees, but the inner pavement was open to the sky. Paul studied the problem as he lounged along under the trees. He had seen the palace before, of course, but now he was looking at it with different eyes. Then it had been almost a joke, the last left-over of Boyo's crazy rule. Now it was a target, a fortress held by an enemy, a place he had somehow to attack by guile or force.

Force was hopeless, he could see at once. There were tanks on the green lawns now, and gun-emplacements sited so that their fire could sweep the avenues, but it would never have been easy, even without those. The moat was a good ten yards wide. At its outer edge it brimmed almost level with the paving, but on the inner side the mound on which the palace stood rose from a four-foot wall. Groups of soldiers were at work here, digging out squares of turf, laying grey plastic oblongs into the holes and smoothing the grass back. Mines.

Retractable footbridges spanned the moat in three places, but the one permanent entrance was a stone bridge that led through iron gates on to double curving driveways up to the pillared portico beneath the tower. Here gangs of workmen had been shovelling soil against the sandbags of the gun-emplacements and raking it into smooth slopes, but now were resting on the grass. There was an officer in charge. The morning was getting hot, so Paul lay down in the shade of the acacias as though he'd decided to have an early siesta and watched what was happening through half-closed eyes.

Soon a shabby truck drove over the bridge and up to the gate. A sentry raised the painted pole and the truck drove on and stopped between the two emplacements. A man dressed like a farmer climbed out, powered the tail-gate and started to unpack his load, which turned out to be a lot of small bushes, in flower, and some spiky yuccas and cannas. The officer strode over, inspected the plants and made angry gestures. The man shrugged, carried a pink-flowered bush over to the right emplacement, scooped a hole in the fresh earth with his hands, dumped the bush in it and stood back to look at the result. The officer, now furious, started to shout at him.

They were trying to hide the gun-emplacements, of course. They were demolishing the road-blocks in the avenues. The Organization of African Unity was sending observers to Dangoum to see if they could still hold a conference here next month without seeming to be approving of a coup by a blood-thirsty dictator, so Basso-Iskani was putting on a show for them. Plant a few flowers in front of your machine-guns and the observers will smile at the pretty colours and pretend not to notice the gleam of steel behind.

Watching the scene on the mound Paul didn't at first notice the soldiers coming. There were two of them. They must have come out of the side-gate and over the footbridge he'd used himself when he'd come to the palace as a tourist. Now they were marching towards him, in step, crossing the road. They wore purple berets and clean, well-kept uniforms. Their boots shone.

He watched at first between his eyelashes, pretending still to be sleeping, but as soon as he heard the crunch of their boots he sat up, trying to look innocent and bewildered, then stood. The men had unhooked their long truncheons from their belts. Paul began to back away, hands up, pleading, but they strode straight at him and the nearer one suddenly swung his truncheon in a low arc, cracking him viciously across his shins and knocking his feet from under him. Pain lashed through his skull as he fell, but he managed to roll as he hit the ground, so that the next blow missed. He was twisting back on to his feet when a truncheon belted into his shoulders shoving him forwards and almost down again. Then he was running, close to the line of trees, jinking between the trunks. A shout, but he didn't slow or turn. They'd have their guns up by now, but the curving line of trees covered him and it was too hot for them to bother to run. He raced across the next avenue and didn't stop or look back until he'd reached the one beyond. When he did he saw them marching back to the palace, unhurried, swinging their truncheons.

It was the avenue he had come up by. The soldier was still watching the work at the road-block. He'd finished the cigar-butt.

'What hit you, son?' he said.

'Soldiers. I was only having a rest under the trees.'

'You're all right. Last fellow tried that, they kicked him unconscious. Bloody purple-hats. One day they'll get what's coming to them.'

Paul grunted and limped on. A couple of blocks further he stopped and looked back. Head, shoulders and legs were all still burning with pain and the taste of vomit came and went in his throat. It was the sort of thing you had to get used to in a war. You met heavier forces, you took casualties, you retreated and struggled back to base. Then you tried again, some other way.

Up on its mound the palace glittered in the sun.

*OK*, thought Paul. *Next time I come, I'll bring friends.*

# Nine

That night was bad. When Paul slept he dreamed of Michael, being beaten senseless with truncheons by soldiers under the trees, or riding in a military parade strapped to the wheel of Boyo's car with blood streaming from the back of his head, or just his broken fingers clutching at the grille. When Paul woke his head and back throbbed with his own beating as he stared at the velvet sky and tried to imagine where he might look for friends.

Waiting to fill Efoni's pitcher at the stand-pipe next morning he heard two women talking about a fight in the shanties between people called the Oni-oni and another lot called the Soccer Boys.

'What was it about?' he asked.

'Just who takes the fees at a stand-pipe, usual thing.'

'The water used to be free.'

'Oh, sure. Till the Deathsingers came, and started beating the shanties up. That meant everyone had to get up their own gangs to protect themselves. Nagai got up the Grey Jackals and Baroba got up the Scorpions and Fulu got up Oni-oni and so on. They'll tell you they've got to raise funds somehow, so they charge for the water.'

'But Malani threw Chichaka in prison.'

'So he did. And the Deathsingers went quiet for a bit and Malani had the stand-pipes policed . . .'

'Just meant that the police took the fees,' said the other woman.

'And then, morning after the coup, there were the Deathsingers out in force at the stand-pipes . . .'

'Shows someone knew the coup was coming . . .'

'So the Jackals and Scorpions and the others had to start all over again.'

'Jackals had split in two by then. There's the Soccer Boys too, now.'

'They're a bad lot.'

'Gave the Oni-oni a beating.'

And so on. Paul thanked them. It was something to do, he thought. Better than wandering round the market brooding about Michael. If the gangs were enemies of the Deathsingers they might be enemies of Basso-Iskani too. When he carried the pitcher back he asked Efoni if she knew anyone in the Oni-oni, but she just frowned and said she didn't want anything to do with them. This was a free market and they'd better keep out.

Inwardly Paul shrugged. Everyone will have to take sides in the end, Michael used to say, and the longer they wait the worse it will be for them. No point in telling Efoni that.

'Where's Jilli?'

'She finished that big basket. Gone to buy stuff to put in it.'

He was eating his breakfast when Jilli came back with the basket balanced on her head. A fold of yellow cotton flapped over the side.

'Ai! Your poor face! It's all fat!' she said.

'Just a bit sore. How are you feeling?'

'No good talking about it. I'm a Warrior now. Look, I've bought some pretty cottons.'

147

She had used the process of lowering the basket to hide her face, but as she straightened he could see she was forcing her lips to smile. She settled cross-legged and took the rolls out to show him. A different-shaped bit of stuff lay in the bottom.

'I'd a bit of money left, so I bought a new blouse,' she said, looking at him half-sideways to see how he'd take it.

This wasn't what Michael's money was for.

'I'm sorry,' she said. 'Only I don't want to be a Warrior with just one shirt. Look.'

She unrolled the blouse down her front. It was shimmery green with gold trimmings on the pockets. She looked at him over the collar with her head on one side, pleading for him not to be cross with her – no, for more than that, for comfort, and friendship, and understanding after the horror of what had happened to her family. He didn't need to force his own smile.

'Suits you,' he said. 'My father says it's morale that always wins out in the end.'

'He's right . . . What does "morale" mean, Paul?'

'What you've given yourself buying your blouse. What you've given me, bringing me breakfast. Now what we've got to do is find some new friends to help us fight old Basso-Iskani.'

They rearranged Efoni's stock to screen what they were doing, dug up the AK, laid it in the bottom of the basket and covered it with the cloths. No one could have seen it was there, but the whole load turned out heavier than he'd hoped. As they headed off into the shanties he explained best he could about the gangs.

'Let's try the Grey Jackals first,' he said.

They asked the way to a stand-pipe and waited for a moment when the men who controlled it weren't busy, but no such moment came. The men were as tense as fighters on a raid, and the people in the long queue were jumpy too. Between the crowded shacks the dusty used air seemed thick and oily, like the air in a village where petrol has been sprinkled on the huts, ready for the touch of flame. The Jackals carried clubs and wore grey T-shirts. Paul found one standing alone watching a corner where three lanes funnelled in towards the stand-pipe.

'Please . . .' he began.

'You want water?'

'No, but . . .'

'Then clear out.'

'But . . .'

Paul ducked as the club lashed sideways. He backed away, and perhaps would have tried again, but at that moment there was a whoop from behind him, beyond the stand-pipe, and cries, and crashes. The man looked past him, gripped his club and rushed to join the fight, while the queue scattered. The attackers, a tight group of young men with strips of red cloth round their necks, like scarves, had driven the Jackals from the pipe, but other Jackals came hurrying up and joined in.

Beside Paul a large woman turned to watch with a sigh.

'What's it about?' said Paul.

'Soccer Boys wanting to take over.'

'Aren't they Naga too?'

'Sure. The Jackals came first, see. They're all passwords and secret ceremonies and doing things the way their grandads did. Some of the young ones got

149

impatient and broke off to form the Soccer Boys. They're pretty wild. It's sons against fathers, see. Men! They spend more time beating each other up than they do keeping the Deathsingers off our backs.'

She spat at the stupidity of it and sat down to wait for the fight to end so that she could collect her water.

'How do I get to talk to the Jackals?'

'You don't, not unless you know the passwords.'

'What about the Soccer Boys?'

'Don't you touch them. They're wild. But I did hear some of them hang around Ishmael's, over in Queensville.'

The Soccer Boys retreated after a while, in good order, and the queue reformed, but the Jackals stayed tense and suspicious, and it was the same at other stand-pipes. He tried letting Jilli make the first approach, and one or two men seemed ready to chat her up, but then laughed contemptuously when she began to explain in her smattered English what she wanted, and if Paul joined in they assumed he was a Soccer Boy spy and drove him off with their clubs.

He got nowhere at all that day, nor the next when with Jilli's help he tried among the Fulu shanties. Despite her smiles and wheedles no one there would admit to even having heard of the Oni-oni. On the third morning he went off alone to the area called Queensville, and found Ishmael's bar. There were a couple of young men drinking outside, not wearing red scarves but having the stance and swagger of men ready to fight.

'Know anyone in the Soccer Boys?' he asked.

'Maybe. You going to buy us a drink?'

'Maybe. You going to help me talk to the Soccer Boys?'

'What d'you want?'

'Find someone who'll help me get Michael Kagomi out of jail.'

'That black Englishman! He's no good. Better where he is. Listen. Basso-Iskani's doing just fine, hacking out the old bush, clearing the ground, messing around like a mad ox. Give him his head and before long everything's going to fall apart, and then we'll take over and put it back together how we want.'

Back at base camp there'd been fighters who talked like that. Our next enemy, Michael had said. Paul turned away without a word and started back towards the market. Queensville, it struck him, was the worst area he'd seen among the shanties, the faces both angrier and duller, the smell of hopelessness in the air almost as strong as the smells of rot and dirt. But in any case there was no help for him among the shanties. All those people! They should have been a great power, a pressure, a torrent to sweep Basso-Iskani and his soldiers away, but they lay here rotting and listless, hundreds of thousands of meaningless lives, like the marshes below Tsheba. He reached the market far more deeply depressed than he had been when the soldiers had beaten him up at the Circus.

Jilli had bought a mess of okra and peppers, which he was sharing with her after the midday rest when through the stir of the waking market they heard a woman's voice coming towards them, calling some message.

'It's Madam Ga,' said Jilli. 'She's boss of the blanket-weavers. She's a strong woman!'

Soon she came striding past, big as a tall man, with a powerful dark face like carved wood. She had a

151

black gum-ring in her hair and wore a loose crimson robe.

'Come to the stand-pipes, everyone!' she was shouting. 'The Deathsingers are trying to take them over!'

Clamour broke out in her wake. The Fulu women thronged together, shrilling outrage and fear. Off to the right the hammers of the coppersmiths fell silent and the big gong began its booming groan. Jilli jumped to her feet.

'We're going, aren't we?' she said.

Paul shrugged. He wasn't interested in the stand-pipe war. It was a diversion, preventing people seeing what really counted. Soccer Boys against Jackals, Deathsingers against the market, what did it matter?

'Oh, Paul!' said Jilli. 'We must go. This market's the best thing in Dangoum. We don't want Deathsingers here!'

It was what Michael used to say – the market was an image of the kind of Africa he wanted. The Fulu women were still arguing but Efoni seemed to be winning. She wouldn't want to become involved. If she had to pay a few gurai for water, she'd grumble and pay. But other traders had left their stalls and were moving towards the nearest stand-pipe. Paul rose, tucked his own basket in under a pile of Efoni's, and joined the stream with Jilli.

Soon the alley between the stalls was jammed solid with people, but wriggling under the trestles on hands and knees they made their way forward and came out at the edge of a wide ring of people round the stand-pipe. In the centre stood a dozen men carrying long police-truncheons and wearing blue T-shirts stencilled with music. One of them was haranguing the crowd through a loudhailer, but the crowd were yelling back and the market loudspeakers were blaring close by, so he couldn't be heard. Two women lay inert on the ground. A man was crawling back towards the crowd with blood streaming down his face. The Deathsingers were swaggering round, twirling their truncheons, dominant, contemptuous of the crowd's anger.

Now there was some kind of commotion over to the right, as if newcomers were struggling to get through. The crowd heaved, and out into the space burst a group of men, coppersmiths Paul saw at once from their leather aprons. There were only about eight of them, but without hesitation they charged at the Deathsingers with their big hammers brandished above them. The attack was so sudden that for a moment the Deathsingers gave way, but then they rallied and their truncheons began to flail as they surrounded the smiths. The fight mightn't have lasted a minute, but into the space between it and the watching crowd strode Madam Ga. She carried no weapon, but flung out her right arm towards the struggling men and with her left made a sweeping gesture, summoning the watchers to help, then rushed at the nearest Deathsinger, seized him from behind by his shoulders and flung him to the ground. With a roar the crowd surged in behind her.

Paul was carried forward by the rush, knocked down, trodden on, kicked. He huddled into a crouch on elbows and knees and managed to rise into a space as the rush went past. For a while it was impossible to see what was happening at the centre of the swaying and yelling mass. People were crawling or staggering clear. A Deathsinger emerged, his shirt

153

torn half off his back, and three women rushed at him and started to pummel him with their fists, weak unskilled blows which a strong man would have laughed at, but he covered his head with his hands and ran off.

Paul couldn't see Jilli anywhere. He waited, watching, as the scrum gradually loosened and the yelling died away. People were sitting on the ground huddling their heads between their knees or resting back on to their arms. Others were lying moaning. One group had a couple of Deathsingers down and were kicking and beating them where they lay, until Madam Ga strode over and with just two or three words made them stop. The Deathsingers rose and limped away. The coppersmiths were standing together, inspecting each other's hurts. One of them looked as if he had a broken arm. Madam Ga turned to them and began to speak, making forceful gestures. Someone passed her the loudhailer the leader of the Deathsingers had been using and showed her the switch. She nodded and put it to her lips. Her voice came strongly through the music from the palm-trees.

'Listen to me, everyone. This is a free market. We don't pay anyone for water. We pay one licence for each stall to the market council, and not a gura more to anyone. Perhaps you are saying to yourself "I don't want any trouble. I don't mind paying a few gurai for water, provided they leave me alone in my stall". I tell you they won't leave you alone. They'll come and ask for money from you – protection money, they'll call it, because they'll say they are protecting your stall from thugs who want to break it up. But if you don't pay it, who do you think will do the breaking up? Don't be fooled. There's only one way we can fight people like this, and that's if we all stick together. As soon as a Deathsinger shows his face at your neighbour's stall, you go and stand by him, or her. And soon as you hear the coppersmiths' gong, you stop what you're doing and find yourself a weapon to fight with and go and find where the trouble is. Be brave, everyone. Be strong. This is the free market of Dangoum, and we're going to keep it that way.'

There were cheers and shouts of agreement as she stopped.

'I tell you, she's a really strong woman,' said Jilli.

Paul turned. He hadn't noticed her come back. She had a split lip and the sleeve of her shirt was torn almost clean off, but she had that look of exultation he remembered on the faces of the commando after a successful action.

'It's not our fight,' he said. 'It's got nothing to do with getting Michael out.'

'Maybe it's all the same thing.'

'Maybe it isn't.'

She plucked at her torn sleeve and looked at him slyly.

'Good thing I got myself a spare shirt, Paul.'

When they told Efoni what had happened she said nothing but frowned and started to re-stack her baskets with the best ones out of sight at the back. Jilli helped her, chattering, exhilarated – Paul could remember feeling like that after his first action. He cradled the gun-basket at his side, but when he slid his fingers under the cotton the touch of the familiar metal didn't seem to fill him with the old comfort and reassurance. The AK didn't belong here, in this muddled, crowded community. Its home was among the clean simplicities of the bush, where you could wait, and choose your target, and aim at that and nothing else . . .

That evening, when the market was in full swing, they heard through its clatter and clamour a different sort of uproar, yells and crashes and a wailing chant, then a burst of rapid gunfire . . . no, not gunfire, but very like. The coppersmiths' gong began to beat.

'Ai!' said Efoni. 'Didn't I know it? Deathsingers are back – that's them, making their song.'

The wail was louder now, rising and falling, like the chant round a corpse at a Shidi funeral. The gunfire noise came several times. Madam Ga was shouting, women were screaming, the gong beat louder, there were crashes – pots being smashed, stalls overturned. A woman ran past sobbing, her hands over her face and blood seeping between her fingers. Lights flared and wavered as the butane lamps went over. Something caught fire. Efoni was out in the alley between the stalls, with several of the other Fulu women, shouting 'This is a free market! Get out! Get out!' The noise of fighting rushed suddenly nearer.

'What are you doing, Paul?' said Jilli. 'Why aren't you fighting them? Where's your gun?'

Paul sighed, reached down into the basket and pulled out the AK and unfolded the butt, then clipped the magazine in. Holding the gun out of sight, he took up a position between two stacks of baskets. The mêlée to his right was a vague mass, struggling bodies, mostly in shadow. Orange flames rose beyond. There was no target there, nothing you could use a gun for without killing your friends.

The scrum burst, and several stall-holders came staggering down the alley with their arms raised

156

behind them to protect their heads from the lashing truncheons of the Deathsingers, three of them, beating down in time to their song. They had used the music, and perhaps drugs, to work themselves into some kind of staring-eyed trance. They made the gunfire-noise as well as the wail.

Efoni had backed clear and spread her arms helplessly in front of her stall. Now one of the wreckers swung towards her, truncheon raised, mouthing his chant. She seemed caught in the same trance, but Paul ducked under her arm and raised the AK and cocked it. The sharp double metallic click was nothing in the uproar but it seemed to break the man's trance. He stopped, mouth still open to chant, truncheon still raised, staring at the black muzzle of the gun. He was alone. The two men who'd been chasing the stall-holders with him were yards on, while the rest were still busy smashing the stalls to the right.

'Drop your stick,' said Paul.

He let his index tighten on the trigger. The AK had a heavy pull and he knew how far he could go. The man didn't. The truncheon fell and the man backed off the way he'd come, both hands half-raised. Paul gave a quick glance to his left and saw the other two in the thick of a fresh scrimmage, unaware what had happened behind them. Jilli was at his elbow.

'You watch these two,' he said, and moved out into the alley. The man continued to back away. His silence, his fear, reached through to the men beyond him. One of them turned, saw what was happening and shouted a warning. The song and the truncheons faltered. The men moved into the alley to see better, and as they did so Paul took a step towards them. He felt totally in command, doubt gone. These men weren't Warriors, trained or skilled. They were punks, bullies, beaters of women. Hearing a shout like that a real Warrior would have whipped into cover, checked what was up, and at once begun to work his way round to Paul's flank, knowing that one of his friends was doing the same on the other side. Then Paul wouldn't have had a hope, but as it was he had all six of them covered.

The main fight round the coppersmiths' stalls was still raging on, but this little group was Paul's business. A Deathsinger broke for a moment from his stillness, nerving himself for a rush, but froze again as he saw the AK aimed at his stomach. Paul stepped forward another pace.

'Drop your sticks,' he said.

The clubs fell. Behind him a man yelled with pain and the Deathsong stopped.

'They're coming back,' said Jilli. 'Yeh! They're angry, these women!'

There was a rush of feet from behind. He dodged back between the baskets. The gun had already lost its hold, as the Deathsingers had looked beyond him, seen what was coming and turned to run. The two men came racing past followed by about twenty stall-holders, mostly women, armed with tools or sticks. Even Efoni picked up the hatchet she used for trimming her reeds to length and rushed to join them. The blue shirts vanished in the mass of bodies.

'Yeh!' said Jilli. 'They're really angry, all these people!'

Paul slid the safety up and uncocked the gun. Now he could hear that the fight was on a larger scale than he'd realized, and that he'd been involved in only a skirmish at its edge. And the sounds had changed.

The wail of the Deathsong could no longer be heard, the deliberate smashings and splinterings had ended, and all other noises were submerged in a single throaty roaring, rhythmless and shapeless, the clamour of a furious crowd. Market people were still hurrying in, carrying whatever weapons they could find, the carpet-weavers with their big shears, woodcarvers with shaping-axes, rope-winders with spikes. Two Deathsingers staggered into a patch of light in the alley beyond and were met by a rush of newcomers, yelling their anger. When the scuffle was over Paul could see the legs of a fallen man protruding beyond a stack of grass mats. They didn't move.

Efoni came back. She had lost her hatchet and stood by her stall with her chest heaving in and out and her cheek-muscles bunched. Spasms shook her body.

'What happened?' said Paul.

'Don't know. Don't know. All I know is there's going to be bad trouble now. Deathsingers aren't going to take this lying down.'

Slowly the roaring died but the crowd didn't disperse. Paul tucked the AK back into its basket and hid that among the others, then made his way up towards the coppersmiths' area. People were milling around laughing and boasting among the smashed stalls, while the traders sorted through their ruined stock for anything they could rescue. One stall which had sold rush stools was a heap of hot ash. The bodies of five Deathsingers had been laid out beside it. None of the market people seemed to have been killed, but several were hurt, and their friends were clustered round them arguing about the best way to look after them. Paul heard wild guesses about how

159

many Deathsingers had come to teach the copper-smiths and Madam Ga a lesson and got more than they'd bargained for.

He found Madam Ga herself in the middle of a ring of traders, discussing what was going to happen next. Paul recognized two coppersmiths, sons of the blind priest, and a fat woman with huge silver earrings who sold breadsticks and was important among the bakers, and one of Efoni's Fulu friends.

'That was the most they could get together at short notice,' a coppersmith said. 'They wanted to hit back at once for what happened at the stand-pipe.'

'You don't know,' said someone.

'Got it out of one of them we captured,' said the coppersmith.

'Showed him the colour of hot iron,' said his brother.

'They'll come again,' said Madam Ga. 'Every Deathsinger in Dangoum. Tomorrow, or the day after. We must be ready.'

'Couple of hundred – three hundred, maybe – that's what I heard,' said someone.

'We'll still see them off,' said one of the copper-smiths.

'No,' said Madam Ga. 'How many came tonight? Fewer than fifty. And that was almost too much for us. Next time, we've got to have help. We must go to the gangs and say to them "This is your chance to break the Deathsingers. That is what we all want. Join together and join us, and we will get rid of them."'

'You'll never get the Jackals and the Soccer Boys joining together,' said someone.

'Or the Scorpions joining anyone,' said someone else.

Clamour broke out, everyone arguing about the gangs, until Madam Ga held up her hands.

'All right,' she said. 'What you say is true, but we must try. Now, who knows anyone from the gangs, any of the leaders?'

'My sister's husband's cousin is second-in-command of the Oni-oni,' said the Fulu woman. 'I'll speak to him.'

'My nephew's in the Soccer Boys . . .' began someone.

'We don't want the Soccer Boys,' shouted someone else. 'They're crazy.'

'Who knows a Scorpion?' said Madam Ga.

Silence.

'Well, we will send to them all the same,' said Madam Ga. 'They are the strongest of the gangs.'

'They won't listen to you unless you talk Baroba,' said someone.

'I tell you,' said Madam Ga, 'everything must be tried. Who will go to the Jackals?'

The argument rambled on and Paul drifted away.


That night the market was weirdly quiet, because the liquor-stalls had closed down. They'd be the first to get looted in a riot. Paul lay in the silence and thought. If Madam Ga did manage to persuade any of the gangs to join her that would be a chance for him to make contact with them. He'd put off trying to get in touch with the Scorpions because he'd known from the first there wasn't much hope. The Baroba had always been fighters, and the men who'd manned the stand-pipe on that first day when he and Jilli had reached Dangoum had seemed a lot more formidable than the other gang-members he'd

161

met, but Baroba didn't talk to other people. There were almost none of them trading in the market, for instance. At least now he'd have something to offer them – Madam Ga's argument that this was a good chance to smash the Deathsingers – and he'd picked up a bit of Baroba from Kashka. That might help.

He left early, before Efoni and Jilli had arrived, and made his way back through the shanties to the stand-pipe where he'd first bought water from the Scorpions. The three men controlling the tap looked tense and wary – Paul had heard there'd been at least one attempt by the Deathsingers in the past few nights to win it back – but there was no point in talking to them. From his study of the Naga gangs Paul guessed the form. Someone more important would be doing the rounds soon, checking that everything was in order.

After half an hour a light truck came nosing between the huts and stopped. The driver stayed in his seat while the two passengers got out and strolled towards the stand-pipe. Both wore battle fatigues, with berets, and had the savage Baroba knives hanging at their belts. The scarlet scorpion was painted on their foreheads. The men at the pipe saluted and a discussion began. Paul moved across till he was between the stand-pipe and the truck and waited for the men to come back. When they did so he stepped in front of them and gave them the formal Baroba greeting to a chief.

'I see the black lion.'

The larger of the two men laughed and said something to the other, too quick for Paul to follow, then added, 'You're not Baroba, boy.'

'My friend Kashka Anka taught me to say this,' said Paul. 'I ran with him from Tsheba.'

The men had begun to move towards the truck again, but they stopped.

'What happened at Tsheba?' said the large man.

Paul had to drop into Naga to answer. At the change of language the men's faces froze, but they listened till he'd finished and then strode on without a word. Paul trotted beside them.

'Something else,' he said. 'The Deathsingers came last night to the market to punish some of the people for not letting them take over the stand-pipes. We drove them off, but they'll be coming back . . .'

The men climbed into the truck.

'Nothing to do with us,' said the large man. 'You Naga and Fulu and Issi can look after the market.'

The driver started the engine.

'I'm not Naga,' shouted Paul. 'I'm Nagala. And so are you!'

As the driver put the truck into gear the large man laid his hand on the lever and nudged it back into neutral.

'Who taught you to say that?' he asked.

'My father, Michael Kagomi. It's true.'

'Yes, I've heard him say it. He hasn't got a wife.'

'I was in his commando and he made me his son. But you know him? You know where he is?'

The man shook his head.

'The DDA have got him somewhere, along with my cousin and the others. But I'm afraid that doesn't mean the market's anything to do with us.'

'If my father was here he'd tell you it's your best chance to break the Deathsingers. They'll be bringing everybody they've got, but the market people are

163

ready to fight, and they're getting the Jackals and the Oni-oni to help . . .'

'Slower. Go back to the beginning. What happened?'

Paul explained. The man gave no sign of what he thought but grunted when Paul had finished and swung round and spoke to the man in the rear of the truck. There was a brief discussion and the second man got out and went back to the standpipe.

'Get in, boy,' said the large man.

As the truck wriggled and bounced towards the market he took off his jacket and used its sleeve to wipe the scorpion symbol from his forehead, then laid his knife, beret and belt on the floor and covered them with the jacket. When the truck stopped at the edge of the market he climbed out and walked with a loping slouch beside Paul, looking like anyone else in his singlet and fatigue trousers. They found Madam Ga and her council sitting in a circle under a canopy by one of the coppersmith's forges. She was clearly the leader, but there were two newcomers, a pale-skinned Fulu man in a peculiar wide-brimmed hat and a Naga in a grey T-shirt. The big Baroba straightened from his slouch and became a presence, a leader like Madam Ga. The council stopped their talk and turned.

'Good morning,' he said. 'I am Major Dasu. Perhaps you have heard of me. I believe you're having trouble with the Deathsingers.'

The two strangers rose to their feet, wary as hunters. Major Dasu shook hands with them, unsmiling, and then with the rest.

'May I join your talk?' he said.

'We were told the Scorpions wouldn't help,' said Madam Ga.

'Didn't come from me,' said Major Dasu. 'I knew there'd been fighting, then this boy came and told me what it was about. Now I'm prepared to discuss with you whether it is to our advantage to co-operate.'

A few of the others glanced at Paul for a moment with a look of puzzlement, but it obviously didn't matter to them how Major Dasu had got there, now that he'd come. Indeed, while the Major was settling into the circle one of them gestured to Paul to leave, so he made his way back to Efoni's stall. The market was still quiet, with a feeling of waiting and tension. Some of the stalls were empty, and the stall-holders absent. The ones who had come were displaying far less stock than usual.

Jilli wasn't there, but he'd hardly checked that his gun was where he'd left it when he saw her staggering up the alley with Efoni's pitcher and their own flask both brim full.

'I think there's trouble coming,' she said. 'I've bought plenty of food, OK?'

He was still eating when a shadow fell across him. It was Major Dasu.

'You've got a gun, boy,' he said.

'Yes.'

'Give it to me. Guns are not for children.'

Paul stayed where he was, sitting cross-legged in the dust.

'I'm not a child,' he said calmly. 'I'm a Warrior. Michael Kagomi is my father. I was with him three years in the bush, at Kumin Bridge, and when we took Tala, and the ambush at Fos. Now he is in

165

prison in Dangoum and I've come to get him out. My gun is for that.'

'How many rounds have you got?'

'Eighteen.'

'Basso-Iskani has a battalion of his own guard at the palace, and regiments in other barracks, and tanks and aeroplanes. What will you do with eighteen rounds?'

'It will be enough.'

Paul nodded confidently and looked Major Dasu straight in the eyes. Major Dasu looked back at him, like an equal.

'All right,' he said, 'you can keep your gun for that. Keep it hidden. Keep it out of the way. You're not to use it against the Deathsingers. You're not the only fellow with a gun. We've got a few left over from the amnesty and so I guess have the others, but as soon as any of us starts shooting the army will give the Deathsingers all they want and we'll have to get our-selves more guns to fight back and after that it'll be mortars and rockets and the army will join in and all you'll have left is rubble and dead bodies. Even the Soccer Boys know this. Even the Deathsingers. Got it?'

'Yes, sir.'

'Right. I've a job for you. Deathsingers will be coming back tonight – they've seen their dead, and their leaders won't be able to hold them. They'll have a drink or two first, because that's their way, so I want you down at the liquor-stalls . . .'

'Liquor-stalls won't open if there's going to be trouble.'

'Deathsingers will make them open. Soon as they're drunk enough they'll move in on the coppersmiths,

166

but they'll find the Oni-oni and the Jackals waiting for them. Then, when they're good and stuck into that my people will come in and take them from the rear. Your job is to bring the word when the Deathsingers start moving up from the liquor-stalls. Come with me.'

'Jilli'd best come too.'

'Jilli?'

At the sound of her name she uncoiled from where she'd been dozing among the baskets and stood up, bashful with sleep, in her new green shirt. Major Dasu's eyebrows rose. Though Paul knew from Kashka how the Baroba men regarded women he felt angry. Without Jilli he'd be dead by now, and Kashka too. She was part of what he had done and endured.

'I tell you, she is a Warrior, same as me,' he said.

'All right,' said Major Dasu, indifferent.

He led them a short way into the shanties and stopped by a beer-bar.

'OK,' he said. 'See that Coke poster? There'll be a couple of lads there playing flick-bone. You say to the one in the yellow shirt that his brother's house is on fire. That's all. After that you just keep out of trouble. OK?'

'OK,' said Paul. 'Let the black lion roar.'

'He will.'

Major Dasu slouched off to his truck and drove away.

As they made their way down through the market the hot noon air seemed heavier and stiller than usual. The music still blared away, but the other noises were different – few of the traders were sleeping, and many sat in groups, smoking and talking in low voices. Paul himself felt listless and uncertain, longing for the clean air and clear purposes of the bush. The basket weighed on his head. The gun was no use here, on this mission, but he couldn't have risked leaving it among Efoni's inflammable stock.

A drowsy woman sold them lemonade and they settled in a place from which they could see several liquor-stalls, where they dozed in turn. Nothing happened for a good two hours, then Jilli nudged Paul's side and woke him.

'Men coming,' she muttered.

Two traders appeared with a bottle-stacked barrow, and a third man strolling arrogantly beside them. He watched while the traders opened a stall and stacked the bottles on to their trestle. Before they'd finished a similar team had arrived, and then two more, and by now there were customers drifting in in two and threes, buying drinks and settling into groups. Hours before normal the liquor-stalls were busy. The customers sat on the ground, a dozen men together, and talked among themselves with anger in their gestures. In one group a man jumped to his feet and performed the sort of boast-chant Fodo sometimes used to do before action, with a foot-stamping dance to the rhythm of this friends' handclaps.

Paul was wondering whether it was worth the risk of wandering along the stalls and counting the drinkers when a tall thin man in a fawn suit strolled up and squatted down with a group. They stopped their talk to listen to him while he drew shapes in the dust, the way Michael would do to explain a plan of attack. He answered a few questions, gesturing directions with his hands, and moved on to the next group.

For the first time for several days Paul felt a stir of excitement. The man's face was in shadow under the brim of his straw hat, but his movements had the same spider-limbed jerkiness as those of the watcher at the bar on Curzon Street. The suit was the same. So the struggle for power in the market might have something to do with Michael, after all.

He bought a twist of mu-nuts, which they nibbled slowly. Time passed. Then an army truck backed in by the liquor-stalls and two soldiers unloaded wrapped packages, some soft and shapeless and others hard and narrow – blue T-shirts and bundles of truncheons, Paul guessed. They shared them out among the groups of drinkers who rose to their feet and started to move off up separate alleys.

'I'll go and find those fellows by the Coke sign, shall I?' said Jilli. 'That way you can stay and see what they do.'

'OK,' said Paul. 'Wish we'd had you with us in the bush, Jilli.'

She laughed and strolled dreamily away, spitting the mu-shells over her shoulder as if going nowhere special. Any commando would have been glad of her, he thought – she'd known without telling that this was why Warriors worked in pairs, one to keep watch while the other reported. Oh for the day when Michael could meet her! Perhaps he'd make her his daughter. That would be great . . .

The Deathsingers were easy to follow. The market sounds changed as they went by, laughter and argument dying into silence and rising back to mutters of alarm once they'd past. The group Paul had chosen elbowed their way through a crowd of young men who'd gathered round a music-stall (the word seemed to get round in minutes whenever a trader had a fresh consignment of tapes, and fans flocked in from all over Dangoum). One of the shoppers must have protested at being pushed. There was an explosion of violence, too quick to follow, but ending with the Deathsingers swaggering on while the music-lovers crowded round two of their friends who lay on the ground, writhing and moaning.

The group Paul was following stopped among the leather-sellers. Two of them looked at their watches. Others picked over a pile of goat-hides, obviously not intending to buy anything but commenting contemptuously to the trader on the quality of his stock. Every move they made, every pose they struck, the angles of their necks, their gestures, their voices – raucous enough to penetrate the battering music from the palms close by – all were charged with an aggressive anger that seemed to flash between them like noiseless flickers of lightning among massed clouds before a storm breaks at the beginning of the rains.

Paul squatted down a few yards off and pretended to re-roll one of the lengths of cotton that hid the AK. He had no plan, but he was a Warrior, his job to keep in touch with the enemy. As he waited the man in the fawn suit came gangling in from the left, spoke briefly to two of the men and moved on. At once Paul's task became clear. When he picked the gun-basket up it seemed lighter than before, as if the AK too understood its purpose. The man in the fawn suit was Michael's enemy, a single, simple target.

Paul trailed him between the stalls to the next group of Deathsingers, who were already sharing out the T-shirts. The group beyond were dressed, swinging their truncheons and quietly humming the

Deathsong. Around them the stalls were silent. The man picked out three of this group and slouched with them over to the palms, watched by the stall-holders. This was the tourist area of the market, the prime sites where the stalls sold carved spirit-figures and chiefs' stools and grass-and-bead dance-masks and zebra-hair fly-switches and things of that sort. The stall-holders were rich and greedy, greatly disliked by the ordinary traders. Paul could feel their fear.

The man looked at his watch and nodded. One of the Deathsingers turned to the deaf old legless man who played the tapes and gave him a violent shove which toppled him off his stool. Another swept his pile of tapes from the upturned crate he used as a table. The man in the fawn suit studied the tape-deck, pressed a switch and ejected the tape it was playing. The whole market fell still. Some hens cackled, as though they too recognized the alarm, the moment before the storm broke.

The man in the fawn suit took a tape out of his pocket and pressed it in. Into the hush rose the Deathsong, a ghost-wail louder than human, throbbing from the big loudspeakers. Faint through its sound Paul heard the coppersmiths' gong beginning to beat in answer. Then everything was drowned by the clamour of simulated gunfire.

Paul looked at the stall-holder beside him, a Naga woman, her face grey-yellow with fear. She was piling grass masks in under the main trestle of her stall.

'Want me to guard your goods, missus?' he said.

'Clear out. What use are you?'

He lifted the basket down and eased the muzzle of the AK into view. She stared at it, then at him.

'How much?' she said.

171

'Twenty gurai. Ten now and ten when it's over.'

'OK.'

He helped her stack the rest of her stock away and slid in beneath the trestle between two piles of masks, where he lay watching the scene under the palms. The sounds of fighting were spreading behind him. He heard a yodelling noise, like the sound of Fulu farmers calling the news along the Strip, and guessed it was some kind of Oni-oni battle-cry. The man in the fawn suit was probably too close to the speakers to hear it, but now something went up in a crackle and roar of burning and he climbed on to the crate for a better view, then jumped down again to listen to the report of a Deathsinger who'd come running in from the fight. The messenger showed him an Oni-oni hat. The man shrugged. He wasn't worried. The Oni-oni could muster about thirty or forty fighters, Paul guessed, the Deathsingers six times that. There'd been about eighty of them down by the liquor-stalls, but they would not have been the only ones. Others would have mustered at bars along the edge of the shanties, to make a timed attack from all sides. It was a well-planned operation.

The man in the fawn suit was clearly in charge. But suppose he wasn't there. Suppose he got taken out . . .

Seemingly without his having told it his hand was feeling down through the rolls of cotton and working the AK free. All the uncertainties were gone. Everything had come together for this moment. This was why he had buried the gun all those months ago, instead of letting it be handed in for destruction. This was why the soldiers had come to Tsheba. This was why he had risked the appalling trek south to the railway, to dig the gun up again. This, just now, was why he had suggested to Major Dasu that Jilli should come with him, so that she could take the message back while he stalked his prey. It had all been arranged long ago, and he knew who had arranged it. Her voice whispered in his mind. *I love you, my son. Love me. Bring me alive with your beautiful gun.*

An easy, simple target. Three shots rapid, to make sure.

He slipped the safety down.

If only Jilli had been here, to share the moment, his fellow-Warrior.

The thought of her checked his hand on the cocking-lever, Jilli before she'd become a Warrior, standing in the rocking boat and craning over the reed-beds to watch her father's house explode in fire. A twist of petrol-soaked rag at the corner, a match, flames roaring through the sun-bleached stems, the tower of smoke, Jilli's screams . . .

The man was enemy. He was everything Michael and the others had fought against so long. But Paul knew with absolute certainty that if he pulled the trigger to kill him those shots would be the match which set Nagala on fire again. *Bring me alive with your beautiful gun.* No. Bitch.

He raised the safety and laid the gun on its side. *You've been lucky this time, mister*, he thought. *But if anyone else starts shooting, you're dead.*

Black ashes of burning floated through the hot, slow-moving air. Beneath the stall something stank and flies whined between the stacked masks, seeking it out. The man in the fawn suit leaned against one of the trees and lit a thin cigar, just like the ones Michael used to smoke. Runners came and went. The

Deathsong filled the air, but through it Paul could hear the smiths' gong still beating, and the shouts and screams, and the roar and crackle as another stall went up in flames. And then the clatter of imitation gunfire would drown everything.

He waited, ignoring the flies, controlling his tension, taut in him like the spring of a trap. Battles were like this. Watch that flank, Michael would say, be ready to shoot on that fireline, creep forward to those ant-hills if you get the chance . . . and then the action was all on the other flank and no one crossed the fireline and no shot was fired as you snaked towards the ant-hills, but your task was still part of the battle. So, now, the man in the fawn suit was Paul's task. In intent poised stillness he watched him, like a leopard watching a grazing antelope. The man was still very near his death.

A couple of market police hurried up to the palms and spoke to him. They were a useless lot – all they did in the market was see they got their cut from the hash-sellers. Now they looked anxious, but he laughed at them and patted them patronizingly on the shoulders before turning to a runner who had just arrived. They strolled away. The runner clearly had good news – Paul could see it in his gestures, and the way he laughed as he gave his message, and the way the man in the fawn suit replied, then pointed up at the speakers and patted the tape-deck. *I've an answer to that, mister*, thought Paul.

Again he picked up the gun, cocked it, lowered the safety and took aim, then waited. Just as the imitation gunfire burst out once more he pulled the trigger. The lovely familiar jar of power ran through his forearm as he held the barrel steady.

The man in the fawn suit leapt and stared at his hand, which he'd still been resting on the tape-deck, then at the smashed deck itself, then at the speakers above, then round at the stalls. As the brief gun-deafness cleared from Paul's ears he found he could hear the sounds of fighting, the shouts and screams and crashings, and through them all the copper-smiths' gong still beating. They wavered to and fro, became louder, and then as they swelled were joined by a sudden crashing yell of onslaught mixed with a yipping bark. The man in the fawn suit jerked himself out of his astonishment and climbed on to the crate, shading his eyes to gaze over the nearer stalls. It was only a minute before the first of the retreating Deathsingers ran by.

They took the man in the fawn suit by surprise, but he jumped down at once and stood in the path of the next wave, shouting at them, ordering them back into the battle. They argued, gesturing towards the fight, but before anything could happen another lot came pouring through, and by now the stall-holders seemed to have grasped that these were defeated men and were darting out between the stalls to yell at them and pummel their shoulders as they ran. Soon if any of the Deathsingers fell he was done for as a mob closed screaming round him, kicking and pounding like boys killing a snake till he lay still.

Now, thought Paul. Now someone will start shooting. They've got nothing to lose. He wriggled his way out to the back of the stall, cradling the gun ready, hoping the rush of people would offer him a clear shot when the moment came. The man in the fawn suit made three separate efforts to bar the rout, but they swept past him without even stopping to argue.

He was so furious with them that the traders must have thought he was on their side as he yelled and cuffed their enemies.

Now he gave up and stood clear of the rush in the slot beside the mask-seller's stall. Paul could have moved two paces and touched him as with quick but unflustered movements he rolled up his hat and stuffed it into the pocket of his jacket, which he then took off and folded over his arm. He turned, edged along the back of the stall behind and waited beside it to cross the next alley where a mob of blue-shirted fugitives were streaming by. His pose was easy, like a sightseer. Quietly Paul slid along between the stalls until he was directly behind him, just out of reach. He raised the gun and cocked it, firmly, making the metallic double click and slither good and loud. The man froze.

'Put your hands up,' said Paul. 'Turn round.'

The man did so. Their eyes met. He looked at the steady muzzle of the gun and smiled.

'Big toy for a kid,' he said.

'Man-size bullets in it,' said Paul. 'Want to find out? I've got the catch down.'

The man's eyes flickered as though something was happening behind Paul's back. Paul tensioned his finger on the trigger. It was pretty certainly only a trick, but there was no harm in the man seeing that if anything touched him the gun would fire.

'OK,' he said. 'Keep your hands how they are and turn round.'

The man let his hands drop to his side and stayed where he was, still smiling. Paul had guarded prisoners who'd thought they could try this sort of thing with children. He lowered the muzzle a few inches.

'Give you three,' he said. 'Then I'll shoot your leg off. One, two . . .'

The man nodded, raised his hands and turned.

'Walk,' said Paul. 'Play it safe, mister. Don't think I'm new to this. Go where that gong's being hit.'

The steady triumphant beat was now the loudest noise in the market. The fight wasn't over, but the sounds had scattered, mainly down towards the lower end of the market but coming from anywhere where the market people or the gangs had a few Deathsingers cornered. A lot of the stalls were wrecked, their goods spilt, their tables toppled, their awnings in tatters. When he reached the area where the Fulu women had traded he found nothing but piles of smouldering ash, and most of the space around was flattened. The coppersmiths' section was like a junkyard. Bodies, mostly with blue shirts, lay around. Women, many of them bloodied and weeping, wandered to and fro or helped others worse hurt than themselves. It didn't look like the scene of a victory.

In the middle of it hung the gong. Two boys still thumped it with alternate strokes. Beyond it a group of adults was gathered, with Major Dasu's tall figure among them. Paul marched his prisoner over.

'I see the black lion,' he called.

Major Dasu turned, let his eyes flick over the man and on to the AK. Paul could feel his anger. The man lowered his arms.

'Silly kid went and pulled a gun on me,' he said, easy, amiable, as if he were now among friends.

'He was in charge of the attack,' said Paul. 'He gave the Deathsingers their orders. I watched him the whole time. And six days back he was watching the

177

house where Michael Kagomi told me to go if anything happened to him.'

'Kid's been dreaming,' said the man.

'That time he told me if I didn't clear off the
Deathsingers would come to my hut,' said Paul. 'He
might know what's happened to my father. And your
cousin.'

'What's your name?' said Major Dasu.

The man shook his head. Major Dasu shrugged
and called an order. Three men ran up.

'Take charge of this fellow,' he said. 'Search him.
When you've done that get hold of a prisoner and tell
him you'll let him go if he tells you everything he
knows about this man.'

'He's got a flick-knife in his jacket pocket,' said
Paul.

They led the man away. Major Dasu looked at
Paul.

'I told you, no guns.'

'I didn't shoot anyone. I just took the sound system
out, that's all.'

'You did that?'

'Sure.'

Major Dasu snorted – probably the nearest a
Baroba ever came to a laugh.

'Deathsingers thought it was us,' he said. 'That's
why they broke so easy.'

'It *was* us,' said Paul. 'Us Nagalai.'

'You're Kagomi's son all right. You don't let go of
an idea. All right. But just keep it out of sight from
now on. Off you go.'

'You'll tell me if you find out anything about my
father?'

'Sure,' Major Dasu said.

178

He turned away. Paul folded the butt, unclipped the magazine, slid the gun up under his shirt and covered the muzzle with his forearm. To account for the awkward posture he clutched his elbow with his free hand, as though he too had been hurt in the fighting, and made his way back to the mask-seller's stall. She refused to hand his basket over until he'd repaid the ten gurai she'd given him, saying he hadn't stayed to guard her stall till all the fighting was over. She was a mean woman. All around the market-people were rejoicing in the defeat of the Deathsingers, especially the traders who'd done no fighting and suffered no damage to their stalls. Paul hid the gun among the rolls of cloth and went to look for Jilli.

The Fulu women were standing in an excited group among their burnt-out stalls, twittering their triumph, bandaging each other's wounds but hardly seeming to notice their pain or loss. Efoni said she hadn't seen Jilli since she'd left with Paul to watch the Deathsingers assemble. By now a makeshift hospital for the badly hurt was being set up, but she wasn't there either. He tried the bar where Major Dasu's messengers had waited and questioned anyone who would listen to him, with no luck. Major Dasu was deep in conference with the other gang-leaders and Madam Ga, but one of his aides helped Paul find the actual messengers. One had bicycled off to fetch the Scorpions, but the one who'd stayed said Jilli had been going back towards the market.

It was dusk now. Paul worked systematically along the stalls, searching and asking. He found her well after dark. At that edge of the market, traders dumped their broken stuff and rotten fruit and other trash for the shanty children to pick over. Paul heard the cry of discovery, the clack of children's voices, the note of both shock and thrill. Sick with certainty he went to look.

The children had pulled her out from the garbage and laid her on the ground. Paul shoved them aside and knelt. There was light from a stall near by, but the shadows of the jostling children covered her and he could barely see. Touch told him that her face was all drying blood, her eyes glued tight so that he couldn't lift the lids. There seemed to be no pulse or breath. He slid his arms beneath her thighs and shoulders and with the children's help staggered to his feet.

'Bring my basket. Two gurai,' he said and lurched towards the market. It was no use. She must be dead.

*It is my doing*, he thought. *Mine and my mother's. It is because I sent her with the message. It is because I used my gun. It is because I remembered her and saw the burning hut. My mother didn't like that. She's a jealous bitch. She wants me for herself, alone. Soon as I'm learning to love someone else . . .*

His right arm was slipping from its hold. With an effort he shrugged Jilli's body into a new position. At the jar of movement he thought he heard her moan.

# Ten

There were no medicines. Efoni cleaned Jilli up and laid her with the others in a cleared space between the burnt stalls. They wrapped her in a half-charred blanket given by one of the weaver-women. She had been clubbed, thrown on the rubbish-tip and left for dead. Paul squatted at her side hour after hour, holding her thin-boned hand and trying to guess her needs, bathing her face or coaxing a few drops between the split and swollen lips, easing her blanket loose when she seemed feverish and wrapping it back before she chilled.

Grim or sobbing, some carrying hand-torches, people moved through the hospital space as they looked for missing members of their families. The patients muttered, moaned, or lay still. Two of them died that night. From the talk around him Paul learnt that eleven other market-people had been killed. Nobody knew how many Deathsingers, and the friendly gangs had taken care of their own.

Tones changed as the night went by. At first the talk was excited, exultant, but later, at least around the hospital-space, the voices quietened, sombre with the sense of loss, doubtful about tomorrow. Most of the Deathsingers had got away. This time the Scorpions' ambush had taken them unawares. They had allies in the army, friends in Basso-Iskani's government. They had power on their side. How would they try to use it?

181

In the small hours Jilli's body went limp. Paul thought she'd died too, till he found her faint pulse, slower than before but steadier, and guessed she had slipped into real sleep. But as he eased his hand free her fingers tightened, so he stretched out on the ground beside her and dozed until dawn.

At first light he went to the stand-pipe. The Oni-oni were in control, but making no charge, and the queue was already long, with the market-people expecting more trouble and filling their flasks early. He returned to find that a doctor had arrived, a pudgy Indian with a turban working his way down the line of wounded, re-setting broken bones and bathing wounds with antiseptic. There wasn't much else he could do. When he came to Jilli he knelt beside her, felt her pulse, bathed her wounds and with his fingertips explored the bruises beneath her blood-matted hair.

'Fractured, almost certainly,' he said.

'She going be OK? She getting better?'

The doctor shrugged.

'You take her now to big hospital, please?'

The doctor looked at him with soft, sad eyes.

'How much?' said Paul. 'Fifty dollar? Hundred dollar?'

The doctor's eyebrows rose almost to his turban but his eyes stayed sad.

'You have that kind of money?'

Paul nodded.

'Thirty will be enough,' said the doctor. 'It is not for me, I must inform you. My name is Dr Singh and I work for Save the Children. I am due to go to Olo tomorrow, but when I heard of the trouble in the market I came to see what I could do. I have no facilities in Dangoum, but for thirty dollars I think I can get your friend a bed in the General Hospital, and for a few more dollars a week see that she is cared for. The hospital is of course free, but in this dreadful country everything has a price. Everything except death. Perhaps what has happened to your friend is the price for something.'

'Yes,' said Paul.

'We will need a litter. I will see to the other patients first.'

'My thanks, oh my best thanks.'

The doctor smiled at him and turned to the next patient. By the time he came back Paul had constructed an adequate litter from the debris of the smashed stalls. They eased Jilli on to it, stacked the satchel and the basket of cloths round her, and carried her out to the doctor's battered Jeep. Paul sat in the back to steady the litter as they eased through the first narrow streets, but when they reached the nearest avenue they found the entrance to it barred, with the cars that had come before them being ordered by soldiers to turn and go back. It was an awkward manoeuvre, and the doctor was still waiting his turn when Paul heard the wail of sirens. A moment later a cavalcade of limousines and outriders flashed up the avenue towards the palace. A helicopter drubbed overhead.

'These must be the OAU observers arriving to see that all is peaceful and beautiful in Dangoum,' said the doctor. 'You chose a somewhat tactless day for your fracas in the market.'

The road-block in the next avenue was normal, with the soldiers letting cars through for twenty gurai. They barely glanced at Jilli. The hospital was a glistening silver-glass tower right at the top of the

183

avenue. Dr Singh negotiated their way in – five gurai for the doorman, twenty for the receptionist to listen to them, another fifty for her to make out a file and send them up to the ward. Then a wait in a lobby until an administrator came to tell them there were no beds free. Five dollars for him, and three for the ward sister – why, there was a bed after all! Just a misunderstanding, Dr Singh. The sister had showed up so fast that it was as if she could smell the money, and the consultant came almost as soon. Ten dollars for him.

Nothing for the nurses who undressed Jilli, clucking over her wounds, and then put her into a hospital nightdress and tucked her into a spotless-seeming bed. The consultant muttered to Dr Singh about X-rays, felt her pulse, examined her head. Dr Singh beckoned Paul aside.

'Dr Anchang is a fine doctor,' he whispered. 'Do not despise him for taking a bribe – how can he live on his state pay? He will care for your friend as well as it can be done in Dangoum. You have been lucky. See how many nurses there are, how clean the ward is? Even the air-conditioning is working! This is because the OAU observers will be brought here tomorrow, this being the sort of thing the government wishes them to observe, eh? I have said your friend was hit by a truck. She is the daughter of friends of mine who are out of the country and you are their adopted son. They do not believe any of this, of course, but they will wish me to think well of them and put in good reports.'

One day if you are lucky, Michael had once said, you will meet a really good man or woman and then you will know that there is hope for the rest of us.

Paul hadn't cried for years. He was a Warrior. Even last night, when he'd been carrying Jilli down through the market, certain she was dead, his eyes had stayed dry. Now tears streamed, uncontrollable. He fumbled in his satchel for money.

'Oh no,' said Dr Singh, smiling. 'I am here to give, not to take. Keep your money for these good nurses, who need it. I think your friend will recover, with their help. Perhaps we will meet again. Goodbye.'

He shook hands with Paul, then with the consultant, and left. Paul found a stool and sat by Jilli's bed, holding her limp hand. He couldn't see that she was breathing, but every now and then a few bubbles would form between her bulging lips and show him she was alive. Other patients shuffled around, or lay and slept. Outside the window, ten storeys below, he could see the top of the avenue, the curve of the Circus and the moat and part of the mound the palace stood on. After an hour the sister, a square, frowning Naga woman, just like a market-trader apart from her uniform, noticed him.

'You better go now,' she said. 'We've got to get things ready for these big-wigs tomorrow. No visiting till day after that.'

'Is she going to get better? When will you know?'

'Got to wait for the X-rays. Maybe she'll wake up and not remember anything.'

'She'll be frightened if I'm not here. She's never been in a place like this. She's straight from the Strip.'

'OK, OK. We'll tell her you'll be back. What's your name?'

'Paul Kagomi.'

He said it without thinking, as though it had been one of the teachers at Tsheba asking him. All his con-

185

cern was with Jilli – nothing else mattered. The sister froze. Her eyes rolled right and left.

'You know Michael Kagomi?' she muttered.

He looked at her, trying to read her face. She'd taken three dollars to let Jilli into her ward – what else mightn't she do for money? Michael was Naga, like her, but there were Nagai in the army, and the DDA. He thought of Dr Singh. Hope for the rest of us.

'My father,' he whispered.

'OK. Come back tomorrow, four in the afternoon. These OAU fellows will have gone by then. The radiographer, she's my cousin – we'll have the X-rays done. And listen, those scum at the entrance, don't you pay them anything. You've got a message for Sister Samora in Algeria Ward, tell them. And think up another name for yourself, OK?'

He thanked her and left. On his way back to the market he saw another helicopter coming from the direction of the airport and settling down towards the palace. More observers? What would they see? What they were shown, of course – a clean ward in a hospital, scrubbed children singing in a school, soldiers helping dig an irrigation ditch. What did they care about Jilli, broken and mindless? About Michael Kagomi's battered hands on the grille of his cell? Unless you shoved these things right under their noses they'd look the other way.

He trudged on. The AK seemed intolerably heavy in its basket, a burden to be carried, a secret to be hidden, a shame – he'd never felt like that about it before.

The smashed tape-deck hadn't been replaced so the speakers were silent, but it wasn't only because of that that the market felt strange. The few customers who'd come were in a hurry to buy and get clear, and the traders milled around in groups, muttering, gossiping, snarling arguments to and fro. The liquor-sellers were holding a furious meeting – they'd only opened up under pressure from the Deathsingers, who'd then wrecked their stalls in their retreat, smashing all the bottles they couldn't carry away. It was the coppersmiths' fault for starting the trouble in the first place. Quite a few traders seemed to feel like that, but mostly they were being shouted down.

Paul threaded his way up to the Fulu section, found Efoni and told her what had happened to Jilli. Then he went to look for one of Major Dasu's men, in case the man in the fawn suit had said anything about Michael. Up by the scene of the main fighting a crowd had gathered, a ring of people watching something at the centre. Wriggling between legs Paul saw that a TV crew had arrived and were interviewing Madam Ga, who was standing in front of the cameraman, speaking in her usual commanding voice, sweeping the crowd with her gestures into cries of agreement and approval before pausing for the interpreter. Paul looked round the ring for one of the Scorpions, but couldn't see any. He was about to worm his way out to hunt elsewhere when a man pushed through and ran up to Madam Ga. The TV people tried to shoo him away but Madam Ga intervened and began to listen to his message. The interviewer, a European, took the chance to come over and talk to the man with the microphone, close to where Paul stood.

'Great eh?' Paul heard him say. 'She's a natural. Shame it's all about only water.'

Madam Ga held up her hands. Everyone fell silent.

187

'Listen here,' she called. 'The soldiers are coming. Don't know what for, but we don't want them here. We can't fight the soldiers. But we can go and talk to them. Come with me. Don't bring any weapons. Don't try and fight. Follow me.'

She gathered her robe around her and strode off. The ring of people opened to let her through and then jostled after her, engulfing the TV people and separating them from each other. Paul found himself shoved up against the interviewer, a bony man with a ginger beard, who was calling out over the heads of the crowd, 'Hey! What was all that about?'

'Soldiers coming,' said Paul. 'Madam Ga going to argue with them.'

'Thanks. Derek! Bim!'

He started to wave his arm to his friends to gather.

'Please, mister,' said Paul. 'You know Joel Funk?'

'Joel, sure. How . . . Bim, kid here tells me the army are coming and Madam Ga's gone off to face them out. Get what you can, but keep out of trouble. We don't want ourselves slung out of the country over a squabble about water rights. Not worth it, just for that. OK? Sorry, kid. No time to chat about old Joel.'

'Please mister, this fight not just for water rights. This be all against Basso-Iskani. He sending in these Deathsingers. I see fellow done give all the orders – he from DDA, secret police. OK?'

The man stared down at Paul, pulling his beard.

'Pretty politicized kids you have in Nagala,' he said.

'Sure. I been in war, along by Michael Kagomi. Three year I done fight.'

'Right. Hey! Derek! Where's young Sonia? Look, darling, this kid tells me this is worth looking in to.

He says the gang who bust up the stalls is a branch of the secret police – is that right?'

'Well, Simon, it is rumoured,' said the interpreter cautiously. She was a slim brown-skinned woman wearing a smart blue trouser-suit.

'And Michael Kagomi – is that right, kid? – who he?'

'He was leader of one of the Malani commandos, and then Minister for Rehabilitation. He was arrested in the coup and is awaiting trial on corruption charges.'

'Right. Let's go see what's up. Tag along, kid – you might be useful.'

The alley between the smashed stalls was jammed with the excited crowd. Dust hung over everything, and there were jeers and whoops and whistles, wave after wave, all mixed with the deep throb of engines.

'This is no good,' said Simon. 'Can't see a bloody thing.'

'If they are soldiers they may shoot,' said the woman called Sonia. She looked pretty scared.

'Not with the OAU observers in town they won't,' said Simon. 'And this lot's only got to realize that and they'll see them off. Bloody hell! Think this'll take my weight? No, there!'

Ruthlessly he barged his way across to the stack of used batteries waiting to be dismantled and clambered up, teetering for a moment and then peering over the heads of the crowd. The awning the battery-boys worked under had hung from a clumsy tripod. It had been ripped away in the fight, but the poles still stood, so Paul put his basket down, swarmed up and hung with his arm through the crotch where the poles were lashed together.

189

Now he could see the army trucks over the milling mob. Three of them, a dozen soldiers in each, their guns ready, pointing at the crowd. But they were uncertain, nervous, looking around for orders. The people were all round the trucks now, arguing and screaming defiance. Black fists waved in the air. Still the soldiers did nothing. A woman tried to scramble aboard the second truck. Her friends heaved her up from below. Three or four others followed. They harangued the soldiers like mothers scolding their children – indeed most of the soldiers looked almost young enough for that, and grinned and shook their heads and made not-my-fault shrugs, like children do when they are bad-mouthed.

An officer was leaning from the window of the cab on the other side, bellowing at the crowd, not realizing what was happening behind him. One of the women was right up on the cab roof now. She dragged a young soldier up beside her, flung her arms round his waist, seized his other hand and began to dance, stamping her bare feet on the metal as she spun him round. He seemed helpless in her grasp, like a straw man, hypnotized. The crowd below clapped in rhythm to the stamp of her feet. Now the officer twisted round, leaning still further, to see the cause of the thunder over his head. His mouth gaped. His eyes bulged. Then someone below opened the door and he fell headlong into the crowd.

Cheering rose, and its roar spread and spread. Turning, Paul saw that though a few minutes ago he'd been standing at the back of the crowd, now it crammed the alleys fifty deep behind him. Anywhere climbable had someone perched on it, shouting news of what was happening round the trucks. Half the market, far more than had risked actually fighting the Deathsingers, must have gathered to the uproar. He could feel their excitement, the surge of power that came from such a mass of people that armed soldiers seemed helpless against it.

The engines roared. Slowly, surrounded and followed by the hooting mob, the trucks backed away. The torrent of bodies swayed Paul's perch, so he slid to the ground, rescuing his basket just in time. He struggled across the stream to the battery-pile, where Simon was scrambling down.

'Great stuff, if Bim got it,' he said. 'Only what the hell was it about? Why'd they send just rookies?'

Paul shrugged. He'd never seen or heard of government soldiers behaving like this before.

'Right,' said Simon. 'Now we want something to tie this in with what you were saying about it not being just a fuss about water. From all I hear Basso-Iskani's a total thug, but what we've got so far doesn't show him that way.'

'Maybe I finding you Major Dasu. He head of Scorpions – he telling you.'

'Not another talking head if I can help it. Something more visual, a protest march, banners with slogans, get it? Hey, Bim! How'd you make out? Where's that Sonia?'

He forgot about Paul and started a frantic-seeming discussion with his crew, but then a group of young men nearby broke into an impromptu triumph-dance and the cameraman swung round to film it. Paul tugged Simon's sleeve.

'Please, mister,' he said. 'I fix you banner, OK?'

'Fine, fine. See you back here in half an hour, right? Hey! Derek! Where've you been? Seen Sonia? Look…'

191

Paul hurried away. He knew about banners – the children had made them when Colonel Malani had come to the camp to open the new school – and now it was something to do, a way of not thinking about what had happened to Jilli and to Michael, a way of joining in the fizz of excitement that was throbbing through the market. In a pile of cleared wreckage he found two poles. From a stall on the other side of the market he bought a pot of yellow paint and a cheap brush. He chose a bright green cotton from the ones Jilli had bought to hide the gun, unrolled it and lashed the ends to the poles, then laid the whole contraption on the ground. He worked out the spacing and wrote his message in tall, thin letters.

FREE MICHAEL KAGOMI

By the time he'd finished a small crowd had gathered. They were in the mood where almost anything would have been a fresh excitement, and the moment he put his brush down two of them snatched up the poles and began a jigging march along the nearest alley. The rest followed. They were mostly boys, a bit older than Paul, and when he managed to get to the front of the procession and tried to get his banner back from them so as not to miss the TV people they just laughed at him.

'What do these words say, man?' shouted one. 'What are we telling everyone?'

'Free Michael Kagomi,' said Paul, 'but hey!'

The boy laughed again, drunk with the dance and the parade.

'Free Michael Kagomi!' he chanted, spacing the syllables out into a sort of drum-rhythm – *Bam. Bibi. Bam. Bam. Bam.* The others took it up, clapping their

192

hands in time to their chant and doing a stamp-dance on the last three syllables. Around them people cheered and clapped. The procession grew, though already they were into the main heat of the day. It snaked its way systematically up and down the alleys between the stalls, and was long enough by now for Paul to see the tail of it jigging noisily down one alley as he was working his way up the next just behind his banner. He had joined the chanting and the stamping, but couldn't clap in rhythm with the rest as he needed a hand to steady the basket in the sway and jostle of the dance. Some of the time he was himself swept up with the others in the boiling energies that had focused themselves into the market and come bursting out in the parade, until all he could think, all he could hear or feel, was the thud of his feet on the bare earth and Michael's name repeated and repeated until the syllables were meaningless as the call of a bird. But then the weight of the gun would pull him down, reminding him of his difference, reminding him of Michael bloodied in his cell and Jilli smashed and senseless in her hospital bed.

At the top of the central alley Madam Ga was waiting for them with the TV crew behind. She made herself the head of the procession and danced towards the camera, clapping and chanting with the rest. The lens followed her and swung back to follow the banner and then the swaying, stamping, clapping, chanting snake of people. She led the parade the whole way round the rest of the market and back to the now-cleared space where the fighting had been. Major Dasu's truck was parked there, and she climbed into it and stood on the passenger-seat, holding up her hands for silence. It took a while for the tail of the parade to gather and the cries and chanting to die away.

'My friends,' she called. 'Yesterday was a great day, when we joined all together and thrashed the Deathsingers. Today is a great day, when Basso-Iskani sent his soldiers to arrest me and the other leaders of the fighting. But we made them go back. We sent them away. We proved that we are a free market!'

There were yells of agreement, cheers and whoops. The chant for Michael rose. Madam Ga held up her arms for silence but the noise went on. For a moment it looked as if the procession was about to re-form and go round the market all over again. She leaned forward and reached for something which was passed up to her. She held it over her head. It was an AK47.

Instantly silence fell.

'No,' she cried. 'I am not going to use this gun. I only show it to you. It is a gun we took from the soldiers who came. I show it to you because there are no bullets in it. Yes, Basso-Iskani sent his soldiers without bullets. What does this mean, my friends? Has he suddenly become a timid deer, who was a lion yesterday? Oh no, he is still a lion. But while the observers are here from the Organization of African Unity he will not show his claws!

'This is why I say to you that yesterday was a great day, and today is a great day, but tomorrow will be a greater day than either. Tomorrow we, the free market of Dangoum, will go all together to Basso-Iskani's palace to demand our rights!'

This time she let the shouting and cheering go on and on. Paul edged across to where Major Dasu was still standing watching.

'I see the black lion,' he said.

'You get my message?' said Major Dasu.

Paul shook his head.

'Kagomi's in the palace, in the pumping hall cells, along with my cousin and half a dozen of the others – big men round Malani who kept their fingers out of the money-bags. They're trying to squeeze confessions out of them.'

'Did he tell you any more?'

'Nothing you need know,' said Major Dasu and turned away. Paul watched him join Madam Ga and start a discussion. The pumping hall, he thought. He'd known it all along. His dream had been true. Behind him excited voices were arguing in English. He moved nearer.

'Now listen,' Simon was saying. 'I know we were briefed to cover the OAU crowd, but we're on to something potentially much bigger. The Ga female has got real charisma. She's it, with knobs on. Dasu's got information that Basso-Iskani's only hanging on by the skin of his teeth – there's a group in his junta all set to topple him – that's why he's so desperate for OAU approval. If Ga gets a big enough crowd together to stage a decent protest at the palace it might just turn the tables, and the new lot will want to claim they've taken power with popular support, in response to the protest, so they'll at least have to pretend to take Ga into account for a while. You want to go back to London after all that's been happening and all you've got to show is an interview with an OAU spokesman saying sod-all?'

'You'd rather get back saying, "Sorry, they slung us out and took our film away so we haven't got a bloody thing"?' said Derek. 'Sonia's a Nagala citizen, remember. They play it rough with their own people here.'

Simon hesitated. Sonia looked really frightened now.

'OK,' he said. 'Sonia gets out tonight taking what we've got with her. Then we've got enough to show, and if we do get slung out that'll make it news. There'll be nothing more here today – they'll all be asleep for the next four hours and then gearing up for tomorrow, so we'll do the OAU fellow this evening – he'll speak English and then tomorrow we'll just go out looking for a bit of local colour and sort of happen on the protest. OK, everyone?'

'We'll need an interpreter tomorrow,' said Derek.

'Just grab someone off the street when we do,' said Simon.

Paul hesitated. He wanted to be part of the protest, to join his voice with everyone else, shouting for Michael's freedom, but at the same time these people were important. They were going to tell the world outside what had happened to Michael. Often during the war Michael had tried to explain that only half the battle was being fought in Nagala. The rest of it was happening on the other side of the world, in parliaments and ministries and ordinary people's houses where they watched their televisions and saw a little bit about a distant bush war sandwiched between a murder-hunt and the football results. He stepped forward and touched Simon's elbow.

'Please, I come interpret for you tomorrow?'

'You again?' said Simon. 'Why not? Hell, Derek, he'll do as a fall-back. Seems to know the score better than a lot of the adults. And he was one of those kid soldiers – we could do a piece on that with him. What's your name, kid?'

'Paul.'

'Right, Paul. Steps of Freedom Hotel, nine sharp. If we're not there ask in the lobby for Simon Fry.'

'I be there,' said Paul, saluting confidently, but as he moved away exhaustion closed round him. He had hardly slept all night, not eaten since last evening, been engulfed in the shock of what had been done to Jilli and then swept up into the delirium of the parade. In a daze he staggered off and found some shade where he lay down, clutching the basket against his side, and let himself plunge into darkness.

He was woken by a movement under his arm. For a few dream-instants he was certain that the AK had come alive and was trying to escape, to go floating round the market looking for targets, but then he was awake and realized that somebody was trying to sneak one of the cottons out of the basket without waking him. He wrenched it away and jumped up, his hand on his knife-hilt. Two young men faced him, looking sheepish.

'What are you doing?' he snapped.

They shrugged and spread their hands.

'Only wanted to make ourselves a banner,' they said. 'Everyone else making banners. For the march tomorrow, see?'

'What d'you want to put on it?'

'Don't know.'

He hesitated. Why not? He didn't want the gun with him tomorrow. The more banners with Michael's name the better. He could always buy more cloth the day after.

'OK,' he said. 'I'll give you one if you write my message on it.'

They were delighted. He had to pencil the letters on to a scrap of paper for them to copy. Then he went to the rubbish tip, found enough strips of plastic to make a temporary cover for the AK, and went round the market striking the same bargain with anyone he could till he'd given the rest of the cloths away. The whole place was alive again now, not with buying and selling but with the excitement of tomorrow's protest. He ate early, then found a place to sleep.

In the pit of the night he woke himself. The market was silent and dreamlike under a hazed half-moon. With knife and hands he chipped and scooped a trench in the hard earth and laid the AK, wrapped in strips of plastic in the bottom. He stamped the earth into place and moistened the surface with water from the flask, making a clay which would dry back into a crust. As he was smoothing it down he realized he had been crooning under his breath, but the words and the tune were lost the moment he tried to think about them. They'd been like a song in a dream. They might have been a lullaby, perhaps, something a mother sang to her son in a remote bush village long ago, before the soldiers came.

# Eleven

Singing, clapping and dancing the procession crawled up the avenue under a cloud of golden dust. Madam Ga was at the head, striding along in her green robe in the centre of the front rank. Yesterday as it had snaked between the close-packed stalls it had seemed to fill the market with its noisy energy and excitement. Today, though there were probably at least as many people in it, it seemed far smaller, little more than an interruption in the peace of the long empty road. The excitement was there, but the marchers had to work for it all the time, cheering each other on. It didn't build and sustain itself like something with a life of its own, the way it had yesterday.

Clinging to the spare wheel at the back of the parked TV truck Paul watched it come. The TV people had staged a breakdown a few yards short of the road-block so that they could have an excuse for hanging around there without seeming to know that something was going to happen. Now they acted surprise and interest and set up their camera to start filming. The soldiers on the barrier seemed only to notice what was happening at this stage. The ones who were asleep woke up. The corporal tried to use a two-way radio to report the news, but it can't have been working because after a bit he flung it on the ground and marched off.

People were coming out of the houses and shops and

199

offices now, lining the pavement, craning down the road to watch the march approach. Soon Paul could hear its noise. Somebody had found drums to back the beat of the chant and improvise fresh rhythms. The banners waved above the heads of the marchers. The crowd along the pavement was clapping in unison, calling out with excited cries, whooping. Nearer now the procession seemed to grow in strength and energy. Paul could feel its joint purpose, its steadiness as it moved towards the road-block.

From up the avenue came an answering noise, barks of command, the rush of booted feet. The road-block itself was only two poles on trestles between the trees – the sandbags had all been cleared away – so the marchers at the front of the procession could see the soldiers doubling down and taking up position in a line across the road behind the barrier with their guns held ready across their bodies. These men wore the purple berets of the palace guard. They stood upright, evenly spaced, alert, with their guns all at the same angle across their bodies. They looked like real soldiers, trained to kill.

The clamour of the procession filled the street. Paul could read some of the banners now. The leading one said THIS MARKET OUR MARKET but the next said FREE MIACHEL KAGGONI and on the line below FREE WATER ALSO. He didn't hear the yell of command from the barrier but he saw Madam Ga stop and raise her hands dramatically above her head. The leading rank – all women – stopped with her and the march jostled to a halt. When he looked at the barrier he saw that the AKs were up and aimed.

The silence felt solid.

'Ready to duck, everyone,' said Simon.

He was standing on the bonnet of the truck with his arms folded, watching calmly. Bim was filming. Only Derek looked worried. He was in the driver's seat with his hand on the ignition key.

'Better get in now, Simon,' he said. 'We might have to . . .'

'They're not going to shoot,' said Simon. 'They'd have closed us down first.'

Two men, officers, ducked under the barrier and marched forward. At once Madam Ga stepped out to meet them. She was taller than either of them, magnificent in a new green robe. From their gestures the officers seemed to be telling her to turn back, while she was insisting on leading her march forward to the palace. The street was no longer silent as the marchers behind began to lose patience. There were shouts and whoops. The banners waved to and fro, out of time with each other. Somebody started the chant. 'Free. Michael. Ka. Go. Mi!' Almost at once it swept through the crowd. 'Bam, Bibi. Bam. Bam. BAM!' They were stamping now, clapping in rhythm, and the spectators at the roadside, and others who had followed the procession to see what was going to happen, joined in the clapping and chanting.

The ranks, blocked in front, stamped sideways, surging to and fro between the trees, churning the dust into a sunlit haze. 'Bam. Bibi. Bam. Bam. BAM!' Out of formation now they began to move forward, not an orderly march any longer but a solid mass right across the avenue, marchers and spectators together. They swirled round the TV truck, waving excitedly to the camera as they passed. The officers turned and ran back to the barrier as Madam Ga was forced to lead the march forward. One of the officers

201

snatched a gun, turned, and loosed a burst out over the heads of the crowd. The front rank wavered a moment but the clamour was too great for the ranks behind to hear and they were pressed forward, right to the barrier, sweeping it aside, while the soldiers doubled back up the street.

At the top they halted, turned, raised their guns and fired. Simon flung himself down. Paul heard the bullets snapping through the palm-leaves above and realized that the shots were aimed high again. The noise of thirty AKs firing all together penetrated the clamour and there was a momentary hush of doubt, followed by a roar as the crowd realized no one was hurt and surged forward again as if they believed themselves somehow invulnerable. Paul couldn't see what had happened at the top of the avenue.

By now the marchers from the market had all moved past and the banners were swaying their way towards the palace, but spectators from further down were still streaming by. A few bodies lay in the road, people hurt in the crush, but one by one they rose or were helped up, staggered to the side of the road and sat down under the trees.

'OK, everyone?' said Simon. 'Let's go see what's new. Round the back, Derek.'

There was still an immense mêlée at the top of the avenue. Derek turned the truck and took it bouncing back down towards the market, and then round by cross-streets to another approach. There was a road-block here too, manned by the usual slumped and slovenly gang of near-bandits. They must have heard the cheering and shooting but it was none of their business. Derek bought the way through for a hundred gurai, five times what an African would have paid. Reaching the Circus Derek swung left and drove in along the sidewalk, under the ring of trees.

The march was heading towards them with Madam Ga at the front circling the palace in a show of strength before tackling the main entrance. Bim leaped down to film the procession with the palace as a backdrop. The excitement had not died down, indeed many of the marchers had by now worked themselves into a kind of delirium, as if they were drunk or drugged or in the grip of a bush-demon, frothing at the mouth and jerking their bodies violently to and fro to the shudder of the drums. The banners floated past. NO PAY FOR WATER. FREE MICHAEL KAGOMI (Paul recognized the strip of cloth). ISKANI BIG APE. NDR CROOKS GO TO HELL. FREE SADUF – FREE KAGOMI (on an old blanket). DEATH FOR DEATH-SINGERS. FREE MICHAEL KAGOMI. WATER BELONG FOR ALL. JESUS SAVES – ISKANI SLAVES . . .

'Your friend Kagomi's getting a good press,' shouted Simon above the clamour of the chant.

'Very good man,' shouted Paul. 'Best in Malani government.'

He stared at the glistening building on its green mound. Detachments of the palace guard were drawn up on the lawns, watching the march go past. And deep beneath them in a faint-lit cell, bruised, bloody, aching in every muscle, hearing only the endless thudding of the pumps, sat Michael. He was still there, Paul knew in his heart, still himself, unbroken. Nothing, no threats, no hunger, no torture, could kill the inner spirit. Oh, if only he could see and hear what was happening, the banners with his name, the shouts for his freedom in five thousand voices, the voices of Nagala! Paul remembered his own promise after the guards had beaten him up. *Next time I come, I will come with friends*. Then he had meant soldiers and Warriors like himself, with guns and mortars and mines to blow up the defences. That hadn't happened, but this had. This was right. This was his promise, kept.

'Let's have some interviews,' yelled Simon. 'Find us a few who speak English, Paul. In tribal dress, if poss – look, there's some smashers there!'

He pointed to a laughing group in blazing-coloured wraprounds with their hair hauled up into a sort of turret and tied with beaded cord. Paul recognized two of them as prostitutes, though he'd seen them only in slinky European clothes before. They'd already gone well past the camera before he caught up and tugged at the nearest one's dress. For a moment she didn't notice, lost in the daze of the dance. She looked down.

'Like to come on TV?' he said.

'TV? Sure.'

She dropped out of the line. He didn't bother to ask if she spoke English – all the prostitutes did, because it made them seem higher-class.

'OK,' he said. 'You come and talk to my friends. They want to know why you're doing this.'

'Don't know myself. Just Madam Ga told us to put on village dress and come along. It's a great party, great!'

'OK, you tell my friends you've come to get Michael Kagomi out of prison.'

'Sure. Sure.'

'Better say you want to keep the water free too.

And don't tell him your job – tell him you're a spice-seller or something.'

'Sure. What's spice-seller in English?'

Simon was delighted with the interview. The girl's English wasn't much good, but she got Michael's name in, and the bit about water, and managed to sound as though she meant it, then ran laughing back to her friends to tell them about her adventure. By the time Paul had found a couple more English-speakers the march had circled right past the back of the palace and come round to the main gate. When he returned with the next interviewee he found that Derek had driven the others off to film there. A French TV crew was already in position, and some Africans setting up on the far side.

Five tanks, wheel-track to wheel-track, barricaded the bridge. Craning from the back of the truck Paul could see their gun-turrets over the heads of the crowd, and the double line of soldiers standing aboard the tanks armed with truncheons, ready to beat back any protesters who tried to climb the barrier. Another row of tanks waited in reserve behind them, flanked by platoons of the palace guard. The machine-guns were manned in the camouflaged emplacements.

'Watch it, everyone,' called Simon. 'If those buggers up there decide to shoot there's going to be a massacre. Wish the hell I could see what's happening on the bridge.'

'I'll go find out,' said Paul and jumped down. As he wriggled his way between the close-packed bodies he could hear Madam Ga's voice, and the yells of encouragement and agreement that rose as she paused between phrases. The crowd was charged with power, the sense of its own energy and purpose. The sun belted down. The thrice-breathed air, thick with churned dust, stifled in the nostrils. All skin was slick with streaming sweat. None of that mattered. This was the moment of crisis. This, Paul knew, was where he had to be, not out on the edge of things, watching it all with the Europeans, but in the middle of it, part of it, heaving against the gate of oppression . . .

A cheer rose and the crowd surged forward like a rush of water bursting through a bank, helpless to go any other way. Almost at once screams began to thread through the cheers. The deep boom of tank engines joined the other noises. The screams rose louder than the cheering. Paul found himself crushed, suffocated between bodies. The woman on his left began to collapse. He saw her face above him, eyes closed, mouth gasping. As he wrestled to heave her back upright the whole mass swayed to his right and he fell beneath her. Legs battered to and fro. The crowd surged again, helpless, and more bodies came down, knocking him flat as he struggled to free himself, pinning him down, more weight still, smothering . . . blackness.

His own groan woke him. He opened his eyes and saw leaves. There was air round his body. Achingly he sat up and found that he had been laid out with some other casualties under the trees. One of them lay limp, with his head cradled into a woman's lap while another woman slap-massaged his legs, but the rest were stirring or sitting up. The drums were going again, and the chant and clapping, loud and strong, close by. He rose, holding to a tree-trunk to steady himself, and saw that the line of march had been reformed and was going steadily by under its banners. He felt desperately thirsty and remembered that there'd been water-bottles in the TV truck so he staggered off to find it.

Major Dasu was there, but not in his Scorpion uniform, talking to Simon. Three men whom Paul recognized as his lieutenants, though they wore ordinary clothes too, stood close by. Paul was still drinking when Simon noticed him.

'Hey, what happened to you?' he said. 'Looks like you met a tank.'

'I been in the middle when this woman she fall over top of me. After that, don't know.'

'Yeah, that was a nasty moment. Madam Ga was still talking with the soldiers when the others lost patience and tried to storm the tanks. They didn't make it and the tanks began to push forward while people at the back were still pressing the other way. They hoisted her up on their shoulders so everyone could see her and she got them to back off. I didn't see you being carried out, so I thought you must have joined in the march.'

'Why she doing this round and round again?'

'Got to do something. It's stalemate on the bridge. She's got to keep the impetus going.'

'OK. That be where I belong now. You don't want me no more?'

Simon looked surprised.

'Looker-on sees most of the game,' he said. 'But if that's what you want. Thanks for your help. Hey! Hold it! You get paid, you know. Where's Derek? Hell! Look by later and Derek will pay you off. And if things quiet down I'd like to do a piece with you about your time in the bush. OK? See you soon.'

207

Paul waited for one of what he thought of as his own banners to come by, then linked himself in beside it. He was tired and sore. His right eye was closing as his flesh swelled round it and the whole of his other side ached with bruising, but almost at once the rhythm swept him up and he forgot everything except the chant, and the stamp of his feet, and the sting of his palms as he clapped out the beat. He laughed as he sang. He jeered at the purple-capped guards, sullen and sweating in their weaponed ranks on the stupid foreign grass in front of the stupid foreign building. He and the other marchers were life, they were joy, they were Nagala, they were Africa. The soldiers and the palace were dead, empty, meaningless for all their power. The only thing power could do was kill and kill and kill.

As the sweep of the road brought the marchers round behind the palace he saw the hospital tower ahead, its silver panels reflecting the glaring sky. That could be Nagala too, that could be Africa, there was room for that. The thought of Jilli lying up there in the darkness of her coma didn't depress him. He could pour his life and his joy out and up into the sky in a magic beam to flood through her and heal her and bring her back to her natural happiness.

On the other side, deep under the earth in a different darkness, the darkness of prison and waiting, was Michael. That didn't depress him either. 'Free. Michael. Ka. Go. Mi!' As he shouted the name aloud with the others Paul pictured Michael sitting like a bushman in his cell, knees drawn up, chin on his crossed forearms, feeling his spirit strengthen as the message of freedom beamed down to him. Perhaps he couldn't hear it with his ears through that mass of earth, but he would sense it, understand it, and at the same time the stupid guard at the door would shiver and feel afraid.

It was no effort to dance the dance of freedom in the heat of noon.

Round and round they went. Boys dipped buckets into the moat and flung the water in flashing arcs across the marchers to cool them. As each group passed the main gate they twisted from the line of march and faced the tanks waving their banners, shouting their slogans, jeering and whistling, making mock rushes across the bridge before dancing back to let the next group follow. The moat-water was too foul to drink, but trucks had come, manned by Scorpions and Jackals and Oni-oni, carrying drums of water from the stand-pipes. At each circuit the march became more organized. Soon there were stewards picking out groups to go and rest under the trees in turn.

Paul left the line reluctantly. He felt he could have marched and danced and chanted for ever, but even before he'd reached the shade his legs almost gave way. His eye was completely closed, and the whole of that side of his face was tender to the touch. His lips crackled with blood, and his body was sore all through. It was nearly half-past one, so he'd been dancing and chanting for over an hour in the full heat of noon without even noticing his hurts.

'You all right, friend?' said one of the group Paul had attached himself to. They were leather-workers, slim, big-boned women from the cattle-herding tribes along the upper Djuga. Their men were famous for being the laziest people in Nagala.

'I'm OK,' said Paul. 'I got a bit crushed at the bridge.'

'I'll bathe your face for you.'

'My thanks.'

She was still swabbing away when a market-woman came by with a basket of bread-sticks which she was giving away, only a few to each group, barely a mouthful per person, but a sign, a token. Others brought round fruit, and spiced lentil cakes, and ropes of mu-nuts.

'This is beautiful,' said the woman who'd bathed Paul's face. 'It is like heaven. Everything is for everybody.'

Her companions made murmurs of agreement. Their creased dark faces shone with happiness.

Rumours swirled to and fro under the trees, group calling to group. Basso-Iskani had hanged himself. Soldiers from Dutta Barracks had mutinied and were coming to join the protest. They hadn't mutinied and were coming to clear the protesters out. A colonel had talked to Madam Ga on the bridge and promised there would never be any charge for water in the market, but she'd told him that wasn't enough. (Everyone had their own list of demands they wanted her to make, from free housing to UN-supervised elections.) The prisoners had all been freed. The soldiers were poisoning the water-supply. The prisoners had all been executed. The OAU was sending an international force to drive Basso-Iskani out. And so on.

After twenty minutes' rest a steward told them to join the march again. Paul found as he rose that he was almost too stiff to move.

'You don't need to come,' said the woman who'd bathed his face. 'You stay on here.'

210

He shook his head and hobbled into the line beside her. It was really hot in the sun, the hottest part of the day. The arcs of water flung from the moat to cool the marchers laid the dust for a moment but then steamed away and were gone. The march itself was quieter now, the dance no more than a shuffle with shouted slogans as they passed the gate. Marchers were fainting all the time and being carried away into the shade. At first Paul limped along, unable to raise himself back into the glorious joint energy he had experienced earlier. The certainty was gone, the feeling of magical shared strength which he could draw into himself from the mass of people and then beam out to Jilli in her ward and Michael in his stinking cell. He clapped and shuffled and called his slogan because he had to, because it was the only thing he could do, and he would still have done it if his had been the only voice and the only pair of hands in the world.

But it was not the only voice, not the only pair of hands. Slowly he became aware that the sounds of the march were increasing, its energy renewing itself, its joy and purpose coming back. It seemed like something he had done himself, by his own lonely efforts, keeping the ember of freedom glowing with his breath until it crackled into flame again. Then he realized that though all round him marchers were dropping out, fainting in the heat or being told off by the stewards to rest, the march itself was not thinning. Indeed it was more close-packed now than it had been, so that sometimes he and his group had to stay in one spot, shuffling from side to side, as they waited for the groups ahead to move on. Opposite the gate there was always a hold-up. Madam Ga was

211

no longer leading the march, but had set up a sort of parade stand there under an awning and was urging the marchers on as they came past. She looked exhausted with the long effort, but still managed to radiate power and purpose.

Paul had worked his way to the inside of the line of march because he needed to see the palace and the soldiers, to cry his cry against them and what they stood for, and not just out into the blazing sky, so he hadn't been aware what was happening until there was a longer and more boisterous hold-up just ahead and a huge new banner unfurled itself from side to side of the march. GIVE US HOUSES. GIVE US JOBS, it said. The people carrying it had their own chant, with a leader singing a long line and the other voices joining in to bay their answer. They sounded fresh, as though they'd just arrived.

'They come up from the shanties,' said someone. 'Lots of them coming now, all down the roads.'

To see if it was true Paul wriggled himself free. As he got clear he heard a shout ahead and a file of young men burst through the ranks of spectators and rushed alongside the marchers waving red banners over their heads to whistles and catcalls from the marchers, and a few cries of welcome.

'Soccer Boys,' said someone. 'They'll be wanting to take over.'

'Too big for them,' said someone else. 'Bigger than any of the gangs.'

Paul squirmed through and found the entrance to the avenue blocked with jostling newcomers. He couldn't see anything, so he wrestled his way to the tree that stood on the corner. Some boys were already up in its branches, watching the march. He tugged at a man's sleeve.

'Give us a lift up, mister, please.'

The man laughed and heaved him up. Yesterday he might have told him to go to hell, but today everything was for everybody, as the leather-seller had said. Paul worked his way along a branch, not towards the palace but out over the avenue. The branch was already beginning to sway beneath his weight before he found a gap in the leaves and could look down towards the shanties.

His bruised lips let out a long sigh of amazement. What he saw was unimaginable. The space between the palm-trees was filled with a grey-gold mist, dust stirred and stirred again by marching feet. Through it, grey as ghosts, came the people, not in ranks or order, but moving all together, a flood of people bursting from their dam, a river of freedom, not like the foaming turbulent rush of water through dead bush gullies after a thunderstorm, but a calm huge onward movement stretching all the way back through the dustcloud down to the shanties. Hundreds of thousands of the hopeless looking for hope. Oh, if Michael could see this, thought Paul, his heart would burst with joy.

Below him a group of spectators, too close-jammed now to leave even if they'd wanted to, were talking.

'Don't know why the army hasn't shown up.'

'I came past Dutta barracks, and they'd got all the trucks out ready.'

'Cairo Radio says there's splits in the army command.'

'Anyway, they'd never make it now. Look at them, just look at them!'

'Scorpions were going round last night telling everyone to turn out.'

'Oni-oni were saying Basso-Iskani was planning to turn off the water till everyone came to their senses.'

'No water in any of the Dungu stand-pipes this morning – that's all Oni-oni.'

'They'll have turned it off at the main stop-cock – make people think it was Iskani.'

'Maybe.'

Maybe, thought Paul, but that wasn't enough. You didn't get a whole city, a whole nation, gathering and marching like this because they'd been told to, or tricked into it. The pressure had to be there in the first place, the longing for peace and hope and freedom after half a lifetime of war. Then it needed only one small thing, like a ground-squirrel burrowing its hole in the right place in the dam, for the pressure to find the weakness and the water to come bursting through. It needed the coppersmiths standing up for their rights, and Madam Ga to make others join in, and Paul happening to say the right thing to Major Dasu, and the OAU observers in town – you have to have luck too – and after that you didn't need to pick away at the dam much more because the pressure of water would widen the breach and sweep the wall aside and let the flood come roaring through.

A burst of laughter and cheers rose on the far side of the avenue, and Bim shot up above the heads of the crowd, sitting on someone's shoulders to film the mass of people moving towards the palace. Paul was glad. This was a thing the whole world must see. He worked back to the centre of the tree, slid down the trunk and tried to make his way across the avenue, wriggling, pushing and squirming between the barely

214

moving mass of bodies. Down here he was too far from the main protest to hear anything except the vague thud of the drums, and the newcomers had no chants to sing, no dance to follow. Instead they filled the air with a steady muttering shapeless roar, like a fall of rock down a hillside but going on and on.

When he was halfway across the sound stilled and was replaced by a new noise, the wham of helicopter rotors passing overhead. He looked up in time to see the black silhouette thunder by, close enough for its down-draught to beat on the massed faces below. It settled out of sight towards the palace.

Silence, as if it had been a devil-sign, a sending. What did it mean? Paul drew the dusty air into his lungs and yelled at the top of his voice.

'Free Michael Kagomi!'

His small voice was lost, like a pebble dropped in the desert. He yelled again and again, putting the words into the chant-rhythm.

'Free. Michael. Ka. Go. Mi! Free. Michael. Ka. Go. Mi!'

Around him the crowd took up the cry, as much for something to shout as anything. Automatically they began to sway to and fro to the call, stamping the beat out. Paul struggled on, spreading the message, but soon it had gone ahead of him, filling the street from building to building, the echoes bouncing back off the glass towers, as the packed lines of shanty-folk swayed to and fro, shouting for their saviour to come to them.

Bim was gone when Paul reached the far sidewalk, but he struggled on up towards the palace and found the TV truck under the trees, unable to move for people. Simon was sitting in the driver's seat listening to a two-way radio. As Paul came up he signed off and laid it down.

'Hi, Paul,' he said. 'Knew you had to be around from the shouting. You're a one-boy Ministry of Propaganda. Come for your money? You're out of luck. We had to know what was happening outside so Derek went back to the hotel to listen in and telephone around. I was talking to him just now.'

'Don't matter about the money. What he say?'

'Not much so far. The soldiers at Dutta barracks seem to have mutinied when they were ordered to come and clear the streets. The OAU are said to be putting pressure on Basso-Iskani to step down.'

'This chopper coming to take him away?'

'Could be. It's a very delicate situation. If the OAU make it clear they aren't going to back him he might decide he's got nothing to lose by shooting. With the fire-power he's got he could clear this lot out in twenty minutes. 'Scuse me.'

The radio had beeped. Simon switched on and listened. Paul looked at his watch. Ten past three. The hospital was right round on the other side of the palace – it might take half an hour – more – to work his way there. At four o'clock he had promised to see Jilli. Through all the exhaustions and excitements of the day the thought of her had stayed in his mind, a dark quiet space, unchanging through the rush and pressure of other thoughts and feelings. How could he leave the Circus now, when any moment Michael might walk free? How could he break his promise? Perhaps Jilli was still unconscious and she wouldn't know. But perhaps she'd woken, dazed and terrified, and all Sister Samora had been able to tell her to calm her was that Paul would be coming at four o'clock.

What could he do? What was right? He was still shuddering with doubt when Simon put the radio down, stood up and started yelling between cupped hands for Bim.

'What happen? What happen?' said Paul several times.

'There he is! Sorry, kid, got to be going. Derek says the local radio's started putting out uncensored reports. That's news in itself. They've got a man by the bridge. The Ga woman's been negotiating again. The officer there says he'll be coming back with an answer at half-four.'

'Half-past four? This for sure?'

'Nothing's for sure.'

'Only I got sick friend in hospital, got to go see her four o'clock.'

'You should be OK. Nothing ever happens on time in this bloody country anyway. You won't miss anything. Good luck. Come round to the hotel for your pay – Derek'll leave it at the desk if we're not there. See you.'

He started the engine as Bim climbed in and with his hand on the horn began to nose inch by inch into the almost unyielding mass. Paul turned and fought his way in the other direction. If Jilli was still unconscious he would leave at once, if she was awake he'd stay with her a few minutes and explain why he must go. She'd understand. She was a Warrior after all.

On the sidewalk beneath the trees of the Circus movement was just possible, but when he reached the next avenue he found the mass of people packed as close as brick against brick. There was no way through. Hugging the walls he shoved and jostled back down the avenue, away from the palace until the pressure eased and he could cross. By now he was almost down to the first side street so he made his way through to the next avenue by that.

This one was yet more crowded, with a line of army trucks stuck in the roadway, their engines off and the men laughing and waving to the cheering crowd as though they were heroes returning from battle. He worked still further down, through the next side street and on. At each avenue he crossed he could feel the rising tension. Anyone with a portable radio had it to his ear and was shouting the news to the crowd.

'Hey! They're telling the truth!'

'Two more choppers come in!'

'Talking on the bridge again – they offered her something and looks like she turned it down, man says.'

Paul didn't stop to listen. He wasn't going to make it by four. In desperation he moved yet another block down from the Circus and then round the long way, still through milling mobs of people who swirled along the side streets looking for a less crowded route to the centre. He reached the avenue he wanted four blocks down from the Circus and it then took him a full half-hour to fight his way back up to the hospital. He could scarcely stand for exhaustion. It was twenty past four.

The steps were crowded with casualties of the crush, some lying inert, some sitting hugging themselves and moaning. Paul pushed his way up. Porters blocked the doors.

'Hospital's full,' said one.

'Message for Sister Samora.'

'Can't you hear? Hospital's full.'

'She told me to come. She'll have your guts out.'
'OK. OK.'

The lobby was packed, voices clamouring with fear and impatience and anger. A few desperate orderlies were trying to calm people. Paul pushed through to an inner door, shouting that he had a message for Sister Samora. The orderlies on the door let him through. Casualties lined the long corridor, sitting or lying on the floor. Twice more he was stopped, but Sister Samora's name got him through to the stairs. As he climbed wearily up each flight led him towards the centre of the building and then out to the glass wall so that as he turned he could look down on the crowd below, the people in it getting smaller and smaller with distance but the crowd itself seeming to grow and grow, stretching away from the Circus on his left far out of sight towards the shanties. He forced his legs on, up and up to the fourteenth floor, and turned into Algeria Ward.

It was full of noise and excitement. All the nurses, all the patients who could walk, were crowded to the windows, looking down, chattering, arguing, laughing. The radio was on full blast, cheerful Afro-Cuban music filling the ward. Nobody noticed him come in.

A stranger lay in Jilli's bed, an old woman with a bandaged eye. Had they moved her? Was she dead? He worked along the beds and found her in a curtained-off space at the far end, lying as he had last seen her with her face all swollen, yellow and purple. A plastic tube led into one nostril. They'd stitched a big cut on her temple and a smaller one under her left eye. A drip-feed stood by her bed, its tube leading to her arm. She didn't stir, but he guessed she couldn't be dead or dying or they wouldn't have bothered.

219

He closed the curtains and went and looked for Sister Samora. She was standing with the others at the windows, and turned impatiently when he tapped her shoulder.

'Who are you? What are you doing here?'

'I'm Paul. Jilli's friend. You told me to come.'

'Oh, sure. Didn't recognize you with your face puffed up.'

'I'm all right. What about Jilli? Is she . . .?'

'Don't know. We got the X-rays but the doctors are all too busy to look at them. Tests will take a bit longer. Can't promise.'

'Has she said anything?'

'Been asleep pretty well the whole time. When we were bathing her this morning she muttered a bit and I told her you'd be coming, but I can't say she understood.'

'I've got to go soon, but I'll sit with her for a bit if that's all right.'

'Fine. Fine.'

She turned back to the window. Paul found a stool and sat by Jilli's bed. As soon as he took her hand in his, her fingers closed round it, and he felt a wonderful rush of relief that this should be so. It was more than a sign of life, more than just an instinctive movement of muscles. No, it was Jilli responding to his touch, knowing he was there, Paul and no one else. Her lips sighed gently.

A voice broke into the music and immediately the chatter in the ward fell silent as everyone listened.

'Radio Dangoum, Ikaka Fong reporting. A bulletin has been issued from the offices of the Council of State, as follows. "Fruitful negotiations are now taking place between the military authorities under

Colonel Tsoro and the General Committee for the Market. Following a frank exchange of views the military authorities are now considering how best to meet the demands of the General Committee without endangering the stability of the state. A further announcement will be made at seventeen-thirty hours. Meanwhile under the emergency powers act all citizens of Dangoum are ordered to disperse from the area surrounding the Presidential Palace and return in an orderly fashion to their own homes".

'A message has also been received from the General Committee, as follows. "Stay where you are, everyone. Don't go home till we get what we've come for. We are winning. Long live Nagala".'

Remote though he was from the crowds below Paul could hear the wave of cheering that rose before the music started again and drowned it. He looked at his watch. Quarter to five. If he left in five minutes that would give him forty to fight his way back to the bridge . . .

He sat, gently stroking the back of Jilli's arm with his fingertips and watching the seconds slip by. But when the five minutes were up and he started to ease his hand loose from hers she moaned and grasped him tighter. Her lips murmured. His name? He couldn't hear, but that didn't matter. The meaning was clear.

All right, he thought, another five minutes. Though he longed for Michael, longed to be present and rejoicing, close by, at the heroic moment of release, Michael didn't actually need him any more. Jilli did.

He started to watch the seconds again. His whole

body ached with exhaustion. Anyway, he thought, they'd never get him out over the bridge – they'll have to lift him clear in one of the choppers . . .

He fell asleep without knowing it had happened.

A hand on his shoulder, a voice whispering his name. The old signals. Instantly he was awake and reaching for the AK, then realized he wasn't in the bush but slumped forward across cloth in a lit room. Jilli's bed. The ward. His muscles shrieked with stiffness as he raised himself and looked up.

'Michael?'

The face looking down at him out of the light-glare was haggard, grey, an old man's.

'Sure. Me. Michael Kagomi.'

The voice was right. Paul rose and flung his arms round him, but only one arm returned the hug.

'They let you go? How did you know I was here? What time is it?'

'Getting on midnight. I did an interview with some TV people. They said there was this boy who'd been trying to get me out single-handed. Paul, they said. You'd told them you were coming to the hospital. So was I, for a check-up, so I had people ask around. Somebody knew which ward.'

'Check-up? Are you all right? What's happened to your arm?'

'They gave us a bad time in the pumping hall. I'll be OK, Paul. Who's this, though?'

'Jilli. My friend. She's a Warrior. She helped too.'

'What happened to her?'

Paul told him briefly, aware that people, doctors and others, were hanging around just outside the curtain, impatient, anxious. He was holding Michael's

222

good hand now and could feel his exhaustion and frailty. Michael sighed.

'It is all part of the price Nagala has paid,' he said. 'All the deaths, all the burnt huts, all the ruined lives. And now your friend.'

'But it's worth it. Jilli would tell you so too.'

Michael sighed again.

'It will be twenty years before we know whether it was worth it,' he said.

# Twenty Years On, Perhaps: A

The Deputy Prime Minister climbed from the helicopter and the children struck up the National
Anthem. He bared his head and stood to attention
while they sang, a small, plump man with a solemn
baby-like face. The tropic sun glistened on his bald-
ing brow. Still solemn he shook hands with the
foreign dignitaries and officials who had been invited
to witness the ceremony but when he came to the
Park Warden, last of the line, he threw his arms
round him and hugged him to his chest, then slapped
him on the back while they laughed together.

'Great day, Paul!' he cried. 'Great day!'

His staff, and the others who knew him, glanced at
each other in surprise. They knew their minister as a
brilliant, dedicated, eighteen-hour-a-day administrator. Even in the throbbing, jolting helicopter he had
been busy on his papers. Now for this moment he
was a schoolboy on holiday and looked ten years
younger, young as he in fact was.

He climbed the timber dais and made a short,
clever speech in English, mainly for the visitors,
telling them without seeming to boast how much
Nagala had achieved in the last twenty years, and at
the same time without seeming to beg, how much
help it still needed. Then he spoke to the children in
Naga, briefly again, so as not to bore the visitors,
about Michael Kagomi and his dream for Nagala,

224

and how the children themselves as well as this National Park were part of that dream come true. When he'd finished he unveiled the inscriptions on the monument, one on each surface of the rough twelve-ton stone pillar, all saying the same thing in their four languages. *In memory of Michael Kagomi. Freedom, Justice, Love.*

After that the children danced in their tribal costumes, a Baroba spear-dance and a Goyu spirit-warning with great bobbing masks, and the Fulu crocodile ritual. The Minister turned his head as the girls snaked to and fro to the twittering reed-whistles.

'Heard from Jilli lately?'

'She called last week from Bangkok. She's fallen in love again – didn't say who with. Her new film looks like being nominated for some kind of prize. Her second cousin's husband's niece is getting married next month so she's coming back for the buffalo-giving.'

'She'll be staying with you?'

'Couple of days. My kids adore her. They're both going to be film-directors.'

'Soon as you've got dates give my office a ring. I'll get out somehow. I could use a day in the bush.'

'OK.'

After the dances there was a simple meal, every mouthful, even the wines, grown in Nagala. Ten minutes before the Minister was due to leave Paul spoke to him again.

'There's something I'd like you to see.'

As they walked towards the edge of the ridge Paul glanced back.

'You don't bother with a bodyguard?'

'Still thinking like a Warrior, Paul? No, I've given them up. Ah!'

225

The sigh of happiness came as the path turned and the view opened below them, mile after mile of brown bush mottled with flat-topped trees, hazy with heat, yearning for the rains. Barely visible below the further hills the line of the West Trunk Highway snaked beside the old railway. Half a mile away five elephants loitered beneath a stand of tamarisks.

'You seem to have got on top of the poachers, Paul.'

'The DDA have really got their act together. We've rounded up the last three gangs practically before they got started. Do you remember this place?'

'Of course – it was the day the war ended. There was a fallen thunder-tree there.'

'No. There. You were only nine, weren't you? Sizes and distances are bound to look smaller.'

'I suppose so . . . Ah, that explains . . . I had an odd feeling that somehow we'd got the monument in the wrong place. I felt the camp must have been further from the ridge – you remember how the men shot deer and we feasted and talked and sang all night.'

'You fell asleep, Francis.'

'But I was there. That was what mattered. It matters still – oh, if only I could tell these children how much!'

They walked back. The Minister shook hands with everyone. His helicopter rose and clattered away. Guests and children filed off to their cars and coaches. Caterers cleared. Paul thanked his own staff and sent them off, congratulated his excited daughters on their singing, stood for a little with his arm round his wife's shoulders, then suggested she drove the children home. He could do with the walk.

When he was alone he strolled back to the edge of

the ridge to watch what the elephants were up to. It was nine years now since Michael had imported the first small herd from Zimbabwe, four since poachers had managed to kill one. In a few years they might start to need culling. Oh, if Michael could have been standing in this place at this moment, Warden of the National Park. That had always been his dream, but he'd never truly recovered from what had been done to him in the pumping hall, and he'd always been too busy with bigger things. In the end he had let the work kill him. That too had been part of the price Nagala had paid. So now Paul was living the dream instead. Never in your life can you achieve every detail of what you desire – and so many other dreams had come true.

He turned and walked back towards the monument, smiling as it came in view. Francis was really too clever – he'd known there was something wrong, but then the explanation about childhood and distances had satisfied him. Anyway if Paul had told him the truth he would have understood.

Paul gazed at the monstrous slab. Twelve tons, and beneath that a couple of tons of concrete foundation, and beneath that a foot or so of earth compacted to the hardness of concrete by the weight above it, and under that one old gun, an AK 47, airborne model, with a slanting gouge across the receiver-cover. Plugged, greased and wrapped. If in a hundred years somebody were to dig down and find it and assemble it, cock it and pull the trigger, it would still fire.

*Not much chance of that. Lie in peace, old friend. Don't need you any more.*

# Twenty Years On, Perhaps: B

With tired but still elastic steps the man climbed towards the ridge. A boy laboured panting behind him – he'd need a rest at the top, the man thought, but there was an all-night march before them if they were going to reach the river by dawn, and if they didn't it would mean a waterless day in the bush. The mines were laid. The train would pass any minute now. A strike like this, so far into territory the government kept saying was now totally under their control, would bring out the helicopters tomorrow with their heat-sensors and their monstrous fire-power, and no movement would be safe. The boy wasn't much of a Warrior, though he was fifteen – Francis at nine had been more use – but if the man carried both guns he should make it. With the war going so badly you didn't want to lose even a boy like this.

It was the worst he could remember. There'd been other times, of course, when everything had seemed lost, but then the balance had shifted – often for no reason anyone could tell you – until the war seemed almost won. There'd been cease-fires, international peace-conferences, provisional governments, recon-struction agencies starting to pour money in . . . but then another coup, or a fresh rebel leader setting up in the mountains with mysterious funds to buy weapons, or an economic collapse and famine and food-riots and emergency powers hardening into fresh repression . . . twenty years . . .

But never as bad as this before. The world was bored with Nagala's endless war. Didn't want to know about the torture camps and the mass graves. One lot of powers paid for the helicopters and tanks and rocket-launchers only in order to stop another lot having a say about what happened in this part of Africa, and the second lot dished out a few old weapons to the resistance, just to keep the pot stirred, but no one wept or felt any more for the people, the suffering helpless people. Nobody outside Nagala, nobody inside.

Where was a man like Michael Kagomi, a woman like Madam Ga? Michael, gunned down outside his cheap hotel in London? Madam Ga, strangled in her own house by 'burglars'? Or Francis Papp, disappeared into a government camp four years back when the last cease-fire broke down? Or Jilli, simply disappeared, long before that? The only certain unchanging presence was the war. *My mother, the eater of people, hungry for ever. One day she will eat me.*

The path twisted to take the last steepness below the ridge. Afternoon lay like a great slab of dusty motionless heat over the bush. Insects shrilled and clicked but nothing else stirred. A mole-cricket called.

He rounded a corner and stopped. A child stood in the path, a boy about ten, naked except for a loincloth, staring at him. Thin, but not starving. Not a bush-child either. No water nearer than the river.

The man understood all this in the instant of seeing but for another half-second didn't move. Something about the child held him, the nakedness, the harmlessness, the clear gaze. Then his hand was flashing towards the AK where it lay folded beneath his shoulder-blanket while his body flung itself sideways and down.

The half-second had been too long. The blast of rapid fire from a bush behind and to the left of the child caught him before either movement had properly started. The bullets hit him in the chest. He never heard the blast, barely felt the explosion of pain. The impact slammed him backward, flailing. As he fell his head crashed against a loose rock beside the path, but he was dead before that happened.

A scream of fright remained after the gunfire ended. Feet slapped away down the path. The child stepped past the body and peered round the corner in time to see the boy who'd been following the man disappear down the path. He turned, held up one finger and pointed at the body, held up another and pointed down the hill, then moved his hands apart, palm down. Two, that's all. He bent and picked up the dead man's gun.

A man's voice called from the top of the ridge, softly 'What's up?' A boy, older than the child, eased himself from where he'd been lying under a bush, stood up and answered. Two men appeared. All three came down the path and stared at the dead man.

'Oh my God!' said one of the men. 'It's Paul Kagomi!'

Silence, apart from the click and creak of insects.

'He shouldn't have gone for his gun,' said the boy who'd fired the shots.

'What the hell was he doing here without us knowing?' said the other man.

No answer, but before any of them could speak a

new noise, a deep, distant wump, barely more than a movement of air. They turned and stared across the plain. One of them pointed. Twelve miles away, just beneath the hills, floated the trail of smoke from an old steam locomotive. At the point where it became sharpest and densest rose a cloud of different smoke, swirling, mottled brown and black, still expanding.

'He got there first,' said one of the men.

'And the choppers will be all over here tomorrow,' said the other. 'We'll have to get back to the river, at least. I'll tell Nanda. Hide the body best you can, get it off the path, cover the blood-marks.'

'But it's Paul Kagomi!' said the first man.

'Can't be helped. No chance of making it to the river with a body to carry. Don't worry, Doso – not your fault. He shouldn't have been here without clearing it through HQ, and like you said he shouldn't have gone for his gun.'

While the man and the boy rolled the body off the path and under a bush the child used the metal stock of the gun to scrape up handfuls of earth which he scattered along the path to hide the blood-stains. There weren't a lot. The heart had stopped pumping at once. He finished and stood looking at the gun. It was really old, with a deep gouge across the receiver-cover, but it must still be OK or the man wouldn't have been carrying it. AKs never wore out. The folding stock wasn't as handsome as a wooden one, but it was lighter, and it meant you could hide the gun better, tuck it in under a shoulder-blanket, for instance.

*I hope Nanda will let me keep it*, thought the child. *It's time I had a gun of my own.*

# PETER DICKINSON

# EVA

Eva wakes . . .

She has been in a coma for eight months after a horrifying accident. She hears her mother murmur, 'It's all right. You're going to be all right.' But there's something terrible in the voice . . .

Eva has changed. From now on she must live a life that no one has ever lived before. A life that will change the world.

'An outstanding novel.'
*Guardian*

'Shatteringly moving, intellectually demanding, relentlessly readable.'
*Junior Bookshelf*

'A remarkable work of science fiction. It has tenderness, humour and passion. It will not quickly leave the mind.'
*Times Literary Supplement*

# A selected list of titles available from Macmillan and Pan Books

The prices shown below are correct at the time of going to press. However, Macmillan Publishers reserve the right to show new retail prices on covers which may differ from those previously advertised.

PETER DICKINSON

| | | |
|---|---|---|
| Eva | 0 330 48384 6 | £4.99 |
| Touch and Go | 0 330 37165 7 | £4.99 |
| The Lion Tamer's Daughter | 0 330 37164 9 | £4.99 |
| *The Kin* | | |
| Suth's Story | 0 330 37310 2 | £4.99 |
| Noli's Story | 0 330 37311 0 | £4.99 |
| Ko's Story | 0 330 37312 9 | £4.99 |
| Mana's Story | 0 330 37313 7 | £4.99 |
| The Kin (4 books in 1) | 0 330 39225 5 | £6.99 |

All Macmillan titles can be ordered at your local bookshop or are available by post from:

**Book Service by Post
PO Box 29, Douglas, Isle of Man IM99 1BQ**

Credit cards accepted. For details:
Telephone: 01624 675137
Fax: 01624 670923
E-mail: bookshop@enterprise.net

**Free postage and packing in the UK.**
Overseas customers: add £1 per book (paperback)
and £3 per book (hardback).